C000060280

Mrs Caldicot's Cabbage War

Vernon Coleman

Mrs Caldicot's Cabbage War by Vernon Coleman is the book upon which the hugely popular film of the same name was based.

You can find out more about other books by Vernon Coleman (including the other books in the Mrs Caldicot series by visiting www.vernoncoleman.com.

First published by Chilton Designs in 1993
Copyright Vernon Coleman 1993
The right of Vernon Coleman to be identified as the author of this work has been asserted in accordance with the Copyright, Designs and Patents Act 1988.
All rights reserved.
A catalogue record for this book is available from the British Library.

CHAPTER ONE

Mrs Caldicot didn't really like the way her husband imperiously banged his spoon on the side of his cup when he wanted it refilled with tea. But she didn't say anything. She stared at the freckled top of his bald head for a moment (the rest of it was hidden behind his morning newspaper), got up from the breakfast table, picked up the milk jug and the teapot and carefully refilled his cup, making sure that she mixed together just the right amount of milk and tea. For a brief moment she was tempted to leave him to add his own sugar but even that small act of defiance was too much for her, and so she carefully tipped two spoons of sugar into his cup.

However, as she stirred the mixture she deliberately allowed the spoon to bang against the side of the cup. She knew that the noise would annoy him. She didn't want to annoy him simply because she didn't like him, but rather because it was really the only way of reminding herself that she had some freedom left.

For Mrs Caldicot, letting the teaspoon bang against the side of his cup was the equivalent of jumping onto the table, screaming as loudly as she could and tearing off all her clothes. It was an act of defiance which thrilled her and which reminded her, in its modest way, that she was still, just about, an independent being with a mind and a will of her own. She had started doing little things like this after reading a book on assertiveness which she had borrowed from the public library. She felt a wave of nervous anxiety enveloping her; tiny beads of perspiration broke out on her forehead, her heart beat faster and she could feel the colicky pains she knew so well and dreaded so much beginning to grow in her tummy.

`Do you have to make so much noise?' demanded Mr Caldicot gruffly, without looking up from his newspaper. It was the first time he had spoken since they had got up.

Mrs Caldicot felt herself blushing and pulled the collar of her dressing gown up a little higher to hide the bright red rash that she knew was developing.

`I wish I had a machine gun,' she thought. `Then you'd hear some noise!' These unusual thoughts had started slipping into her mind more and more often, and although she found them slightly alarming she also found them rather exciting. She realised, with some considerable surprise, that she quite liked the idea of mowing down her husband with a hail of machine gun bullets.

'I'm sorry, dear,' she apologised, not so much because she was contrite over the rattled tea spoon but more because she was overcome with guilt at having so enjoyed the thought of the machine gun massacre. She glanced at the kitchen clock. 'It's twenty minutes to eight,' she reminded him gently and timidly. It was the cricket season, the county side was playing at home and Mr Caldicot, a loyal and faithful member for forty three years, never missed a home match. The game did not start until eleven but Mr Caldicot always arrived at the ground a full two hours early. He liked to be there before anyone else to make sure that no one else sat in his seat. A double glazing salesman had once sat on Mr Caldicot's preferred section of wooden bench and Mr Caldicot had responded by sinking into a deep depression for two months.

Mr Caldicot moved his head slightly to one side, lowered his head a fraction of an inch and looked up over the top of his spectacles so that he could examine the clock to confirm the time. Mrs Caldicot hated him even more than usual when he did this. She felt that he did it deliberately just to let her know that he didn't even trust her to tell the time properly. He popped the last piece of toast into his mouth and chewed on it noisily. His dentures were ill-fitting and needed replacing but he was too mean a man to spend money on replacing dentures which still had a few thousand chews left in them. Occasionally, when he was eating, they would slip out of his mouth and he would have to push them back into place with an inelegant flick of the wrist. This unattractive habit never seemed to embarrass him.

He cleared his throat. 'Hrrmph!' Then he pushed back his chair and folded his newspaper before placing it neatly next to his plate. He sipped at his tea, decided that it was too hot to drink for the moment, got up from the table and headed for the stairs to finish dressing. Mr Caldicot's attire was predictable and Mrs Caldicot knew exactly how he would be dressed when he reappeared. Whatever the weather he always wore a three piece suit, a white shirt and his county supporter's tie when going to watch a cricket match. She longed for him to astonish her in some way, but knew that he never would. His underpants were always white, his socks were always grey and woollen and the ends of his shoelaces were always of matching length.

'Are my sandwiches ready?'

Mr Caldicot had paused in the doorway before going upstairs to dress.

Mrs Caldicot felt like a schoolgirl being addressed by a stern headmaster. 'Yes, sir, no sir, three bags full sir,' she thought. 'They're in the fridge, dear,' she said. 'I'll get them out when I've filled your flask.' She realised that instead of 'dear' she had very nearly said 'sir' and she swallowed hard. She wondered if he would have noticed if she had said 'sir', and decided that even if he had he would not have thought it odd. Indeed, he would have almost certainly liked it. The machine gun image came back and she savoured the sight for a moment.

'Beef paste?'

'Yes, dear.'

'I didn't like that fishy stuff.'

'Well hard luck! Why don't you make your own sandwiches you nasty, selfish, self-centred little man,' she thought. 'Tuna? No, I know, dear,' she said. 'You told me.' Mrs Caldicot should have known better than to try experimenting with the contents of her husband's packed luncheon; the tuna fish had not gone down well, though it had not, she remembered, been as unpopular as the cucumber. She had once put cucumber on his sandwiches and he had reminded her of his dislike for cucumber every morning for the rest of the cricketing summer. He rarely told her what he liked, only what he didn't like. She couldn't remember him ever praising her for anything.

'And not an apple.'

'Yes, dear.'

'The skins on those apples you bought are too tough. The one I had yesterday got stuck in my teeth.'

'What a pity it didn't choke you,' thought Mrs Caldicot. 'I'm sorry,' she said aloud, in a simper which immediately made her feel ashamed and angry with herself. 'I'll put a banana in your box.'

'My brown suit needs cleaning,' said Mr Caldicot, still standing at the foot of the stairs. 'And while you're in town call at the seed merchant's and get me some more plant fertiliser.'

`What did your last slave die of?' thought Mrs Caldicot, who had not planned to go into town at all. `All right, dear,' she said.

While Mr Caldicot disappeared back upstairs to fiddle with cufflinks and collar studs, Mrs Caldicot filled her husband's flask with tea, nervously selected a banana with just the right mixture of brown and yellow in its skin and took the small packet of sandwiches she had made the night before and put them into an airtight plastic box. Then she wrapped two small home-made rock cakes in greaseproof paper and added them to the box. She put the flask, the banana and the sandwich box alongside the folded newspaper but she didn't put them into his polished brown leather briefcase even though it was leaning against the wall no more than a few feet away. Mr Caldicot liked to pack his briefcase himself. When all this was done Mrs Caldicot switched the kettle on again, put two slices of bread into the toaster and made her own breakfast.

When he came downstairs Mr Caldicot finished his cup of tea and packed his sandwich box, his flask, his banana and his newspaper into his briefcase.

`I'll be in the members' pavilion if anyone wants me,' he said. He had said the same thing for as long as Mrs Caldicot could remember but no one had ever wanted him. He did not ask her how she was planning to spend her day and nor had he ever done so.

`Who do you think cares a fig where you are?' she thought. `Yes, dear,' she said. She glanced at the clock as her husband left. It was twenty minutes past eight. She heard the garage doors creak open and the sound of their motorcar starting up. It would be eleven hours before her husband returned home. She sat down and turned on the wireless. On the news station two politicians were discussing Northern Ireland. On the entertainment station a disc jockey was talking about a group she'd never heard of and a concert he'd been to which sounded momentously dull and uneventful. Mrs Caldicot turned the wireless off.

She contemplated the possibilities. She could go down to the Oxfam shop to help sort through other people's unwanted clothes, books and household bits and pieces. She could go to the supermarket to restock the pantry with essential household comestibles. Or she could give the house a good spring clean.

None of these options filled her with anything approaching excitement or anticipation.

Mrs Caldicot didn't really know what was wrong with her. She had never really felt like this before. She had spent most of her life keeping Mr Caldicot's socks in pairs and satisfying his increasingly obsessional likes and dislikes, but she had never before felt quite so unsatisfied by her life. Matching socks had never been something she had regarded as fulfilling but she had, nevertheless, always been a relatively contented woman. With considerable reluctance she realised that she was beginning to feel frustrated by an existence which seemed more and more pointless and purposeless. Worst of all was the strange and pervasive feeling of loneliness which seemed to leave her. Even at the Oxfam shop, surrounded by plump and cheerful friends, she felt inexplicably alone. She wished there was a patron saint to look after the downtrodden, the downhearted and the constantly put upon, and yet at the same time she felt ashamed of her own lack of strength and her inability to solve her predicament.

She closed her eyes and tried to use a relaxation technique she had read about in a book on stress. It involved imagining that she was lying on a beach on a desert island. But Kitty the cat leapt on her lap just as she had begun the imaginary journey to her promised haven of temporary peace, and the journey ended almost before it had begun.

She got up from the table and started to wash the breakfast plates. She wondered if she was depressed but quickly decided that it was irrelevant she wasn't going to see the doctor anyway. The last time she had visited him, eight years earlier, he had put her on pills which he had promised would calm her nerves. They had done that effectively for two weeks but it had then taken her three years to escape from their pharmacological clutches and she no longer trusted him or any of his pills.

As she squirted washing-up liquid into the bowl of hot water she felt a sudden urge to run away; to put Kitty into her wicker basket, to pack a small bag and to leave. But she didn't know where she would go, and she realised with some anguish that this was not because she didn't have anywhere that she could go to but because anywhere would be better than where she was. She had so many places from which she could choose that she couldn't decide which one to select.

She turned the wireless on again.

On the news station a man with a boring, whiny voice was talking about the boundaries of art in the gay community. On the entertainment station an overly cheerful youth with a relentlessly patronising manner was reading out a recipe for cheese omelette and cracking little jokes between each of the ingredients.

She reached out and turned the radio off with a firm flick of her wrist. She thought for a moment about switching on the television but just as quickly suppressed the thought. She could not bear the incessantly cheerful litany of banal banter with which the broadcasters sought to liven her morning. She had long ago realised that the very predictability of their inanity was more than adequate proof that they knew that she was bored and lonely and she did not want what amounted to little more than electronic pity.

She sat down, silent and lonely, and allowed an endless series of irrelevant worries to drift in and out of her mind. She wondered if everyone worried as much as she did about things and decided that they couldn't possibly because if they did then they'd never have the energy to get anything done.

CHAPTER TWO

Mrs Caldicot was in the kitchen cutting radishes into little flowers when two very young police officers came to tell her that her husband had died.

They were extremely nice about it.

`Mrs Caldicot?' asked the boy policeman. He had huge, pink, ears which stuck out at right angles to the side of his head and his face was covered in spots. He was trying to grow a moustache.

`That's right,' replied Mrs Caldicot, wiping her hands on a tea towel. `Is it about my Aunt Hannah?' She opened the door wide and stood back. `You'd better come in. We've been expecting it.' She felt her palpitations come back again and the colicky pains in her tummy made her wince inwardly, though she proudly refused to show her discomfort to these strangers. The worries and anxieties that had been popping in and out of her mind still nagged at her and she put them neatly in order so that she could worry about them later. None of them was important enough to survive the next half an hour.

Mrs Caldicot's Aunt Hannah lived in an alms house twelve miles away and had been dying for over a quarter of a century.

The boy policeman fidgeted with his helmet. He looked at his companion, the girl policewoman. She looked even younger than him. She had a little pug nose, dark brown eyes and her hat came down so far over her head that she didn't seem to have any hair at all. Her shapeless uniform was too big for her and Mrs Caldicot wondered if her mother knew where she was. She also thought that the uniform looked rather itchy and uncomfortable and was glad that she wasn't in the police force. She remembered that when she had been in the maternity hospital giving birth to her son Derek she had been in a bed next to a girl called Brenda who had been married to a police constable. The police constable had given her a hug and a kiss the day she had been leaving the hospital and if she closed her eyes and worked her memory and imagination hard she could still feel the texture of his uniform.

`It's about your husband,' said the girl policewoman. `Mr Caldicot,' she added, lest there be any doubt about the identity of

Mrs Caldicot's spouse.

Mrs Caldicot felt a sudden frisson of alarm run down her spine and she felt a wave of guilt flowing over her as she realised that the sense of alarm had been triggered not by any fear for her husband but by fear for herself. She knew instantly that her life was about to change though she did not know precisely how or in what way. It annoyed her that she could not remember the name of Brenda's husband.

`He's been taken ill,' continued the girl policewoman.

`Very ill,' said the boy policeman. `Can we come in?'

`You'd better come in,' said Mrs Caldicot. Her husband was never ill. He did not allow illness to interfere with his carefully organised life. How, she wondered, could any disease have dared to find its way, uninvited and unwelcome, into his ordered existence. She wondered if the policeman who had hugged her had been called Bert. He had, she remembered, a huge bristly moustache and she had never before (or since for that matter) been kissed by a man with a moustache.

The girl policewoman and the boy policeman squeezed into Mrs Caldicot's front hall and Mrs Caldicot reached around them to shut the front door.

`First on your right,' said Mrs Caldicot. `The living room.' She knew that she should have asked them immediately what had happened but somehow she felt that the longer she could delay the finding out the better it might be for all of them.

They stood together in the middle of the small room which now suddenly seemed overcrowded with furniture. The girl policewoman looked around and Mrs Caldicot looked around with her and seemed to see the room for the first time. There was a three piece suite with floral patterned covers, an imitation oak glass- fronted bookcase filled with book club editions and paperbacks and a smart new Japanese television set on a metal and plastic table.

Kitty, was curled up dozing on one of the chairs. She looked up and opened an eye when they entered but did not move. Kitty didn't mind strangers. No one sat down. The girl policewoman had taken off her hat and like her colleague she was holding it in her hands and turning it round and round.

`He was at the cricket match,' said the boy policeman.

`At Mettleham County Ground,' added the girl policewoman.

`I know,' said Mrs Caldicot. `He always goes to the cricket when they're playing at home. He's a member.' She suddenly realised that she knew that her husband was dead and that she had known this since she had seen the two police officers standing on the doorstep. She wondered whether or not she would cry when they told her, and whether or not they would expect her to cry, and whether they might be disappointed if she didn't cry. Inexplicably, she suddenly thought of the time she had gone to night school to study French. Fearing that her intellect was withering she had tried to persuade Mr Caldicot to go with her to an evening class. He had refused and had consented to her signing up with bad grace. When she had completed her course she had suggested a holiday in France or, at the very least, a short weekend in Paris. But he had refused. When she had diffidently suggested that she might go to Paris with a group being organised by other students he had refused to countenance such a trip. She thought that had probably been the beginning of the end of their love. She never said anything at the time, of course, but she shrank deeper and deeper into her shell, and after that she had started thinking her strange thoughts. The more she tried to repress these thoughts with a veneer of quiet and artificial contentment, the more the thoughts struggled to the surface.

She knew that she wouldn't, couldn't, cry for him though she feared she might cry for herself: for the lost years of her youth. He had ground her down with his demands, his selfishness and his dullness and she feared that she may now have lost her zest for life. She feared that she had long ago stopped being a person with ambitions and purposes of her own.

She remembered the day, over twenty years earlier, when she had left him. Derek, their son, had just left home and she had packed a bag and gone to live in a rented room in another town nearby. Mr Caldicot had come after her not because he wanted her but because he needed her. She knew that. He had bullied her and made promises he must have known he couldn't and wouldn't keep. She had gone back to him but nothing had changed and the very effort of making that one break had exhausted her spirit.

All this went through her mind in a fraction of a moment, and during the brief pause the two police officers glanced at each other.

`I'm afraid your husband's dead,' said the policeman suddenly, and more starkly and bluntly than he had intended. He lowered his eyes, blushing with embarrassment and ashamed of his clumsiness.

`They think it was a heart attack,' said the policewoman. `It was very quick. He didn't suffer.' She spoke quietly and sympathetically.

`Oh dear,' said Mrs Caldicot, who, despite knowing what it was that the police officers were about to tell her, had still been shaken by the news. She reached out and held onto the mantelpiece. `Oh dear me,' she said. She went very pale and felt as though she was about to faint. She felt dizzy and damp with perspiration. Her colicky tummy pains started again, gnawing spitefully at her insides. The boy policeman took her arm and gently led her over to one of the two easy chairs.

`I'll put the kettle on,' said the policewoman, anxious for something to do.

A thousand unconnected thoughts hurried through Mrs Caldicot's mind. `He's got his chrysanthemums ready for the show next Saturday,' she said, inconsequentially. `Whatever shall I do with them?' This irrelevance burst to the forefront of her mind as though to give the rest of her brain time to think. Mrs Caldicot was overwhelmed and confused by the way she felt. It had been a long time since she had loved her husband, and she couldn't even remember when she had last felt any real affection or respect for him, but they had grown up and grown old together rather like two trees planted to close together. In her most secret moments she had often wondered what life would be like without him, and now that she was faced with separation for real she felt liberated but also lonely and frightened. She felt like a long piece of Virginia creeper which has suddenly lost its hold on a wall and is swaying around in the wind. `Should I pretend to be sad?' she wondered. `Am I sad?' She thought about it for a moment. `I feel happy and sad,' she confessed to herself. `But more happy than sad. To be honest, I don't really feel very sad at all. I didn't like him and I'm rather relieved that I won't be seeing him again.' She felt as though she had been released from hospital after a long illness or released from prison after serving a long sentence. Then she felt guilty again. She remembered that once she had taken a job in a department store. He had sulked until she had given it up, though in recent years he had allowed her to work as a volunteer assistant in a charity shop. When making her give up the job at the department store he said that if she had a proper job people would think he didn't earn enough money to keep them. He. Him. It was all he ever thought about. All he had ever thought about. She had hated him but he had ruled her life so severely that she had become dependent upon him. And now she was confused, lonely and frightened.

The girl policewoman returned from the kitchen. `Do you take sugar, Mrs Caldicot?' she asked.

`No thank you,' smiled Mrs Caldicot politely. `I've got ham for his tea. He likes a ham salad.' She stopped for a moment. `Liked.' she corrected herself. A tear rolled down her cheek and she realised that she was crying after all. `Oh dear.' The girl policewoman hurried back to the kitchen to busy herself making tea. Kitty the cat, who did not seem in any way discomforted by the news of Mr Caldicot's untimely and unexpected demise, lazily stood up, stretched her legs, jumped down onto the carpet, walked across to Mrs Caldicot, jumped up onto her lap and curled herself up again.

George and Thelma Caldicot had been married for thirty three years, and in the eyes of those who knew them had become an inseparable onesome rather than a couple. Mrs Caldicot had grown accustomed to allowing her husband to make all the decisions in their life. If they went out for the day he decided when and where they went. When they went shopping for wallpaper or furniture he made all the major decisions. They spent their annual holidays in Torquay because he liked it there and they drove a Vauxhall car because he had always driven Vauxhall cars. Now that he was dead she suddenly realised that she was waiting for him to come home so that she could ask him what to do. She wondered what she would do and how she would cope. With a strange mixture of apprehension and excitement she realised that she could do whatever she liked both now and for the rest of her life. She had been given back control of her own life. And she wondered if she would know what to do with it.

Something suddenly occurred to her.

`Where is he?' she asked.

`They took him to the hospital,' said the young policeman kindly. He still felt bad about the way he had broken the news. `Mettleham General.'

`His brother died on the Edgar Johnson Ward,' said Mrs Caldicot. `And his sister died on the Mavis Bates Ward. You can never park round there.'

`Here you are,' said the policewoman, appearing with a cup of tea which she put down on the arm of Mrs Caldicot's chair. She had used one of Mrs Caldicot's best cups and saucers and this, together with the fact that the tea had been made by someone she did not know, made Mrs Caldicot feel something of a stranger in her own home. The two police officers watched her sip the tea, as though it were medicine which would magically and mysteriously soothe her mental aches and pains. Mrs Caldicot felt uncomfortable.

`Do you have someone we could call for you?' asked the boy policeman. `A relative or a friend?'

`I have a son,' said Mrs Caldicot. `Derek. He's in property.' She realised what she felt uncomfortable about. `Aren't you having a cup?' she asked them both, looking first at one and then the other.

`Do you have a number for him?' asked the girl policewoman.

`He'll be at work,' said Mrs Caldicot. `I don't like to bother him at work.'

`I'm sure he won't mind,' said the girl policewoman. She paused. `Considering the circumstances.'

`No,' said Mrs Caldicot. `I suppose not.'

`Do you have a number for him?' She asked again.

Mrs Caldicot gave the policewoman her son's number. `Derek Caldicot is his name but you have to ask for Mr Caldicot.' Mrs Caldicot had a sudden feeling that without her husband to do the bullying her son would take over her life. She wondered if she had ever loved her husband. She supposed she must have once. Or maybe she just thought she loved him. She tried to think back to when they had both been young. She couldn't recall any particularly happy memories and that made her sad. Why, she wondered, had she married him at all? Perhaps because everyone had expected her to. They had met at a cricket club dance. Her father had been a keen player but her husband-to-be had never played. He'd always been a spectator. That just about summed him up, she thought. He'd always been a spectator. And she'd been even worse. She'd merely made his sandwiches. He had watched while life passed him by and she had made his sandwiches and sorted his socks. They had met, danced shyly together, and that was that. Trips to the cinema. Days out watching cricket. Days spent cycling to local churches. An engagement. And then a wedding, a tiny flat, a baby, a small house, a larger house and then this. It didn't seem to have been an awful lot of fun.

The policewoman dialled the number that Mrs Caldicot had given her. The policeman stood uncomfortably in the middle of Mrs Caldicot's living room and Mrs Caldicot sipped her cup of tea. Only when she had nearly finished drinking it did she remember that she hardly ever drank tea and that she much preferred coffee.

`Could I speak to Mr Caldicot, please?' asked the girl policewoman.

Mrs Caldicot couldn't hear the other half of the conversation but she could imagine it. `I'm afraid Mr Caldicot is in a meeting at the moment,' the receptionist would say. `Can I take a message and get him to ring you back?'

`It is rather urgent and important that I speak to him,' said the policewoman. She gave her name and rank.

`I'll see what I can do,' the receptionist would be saying.

A moment or two later Mrs Caldicot could hear her son's voice booming out of the telephone. He always sounded rather aggressive though he was not a brave man and would have run a mile if anyone had threatened him with so much as a rolled up newspaper. `If it's about that neighbour of mine then you can take it from me that he's a liar,' she heard him say. `That tree was hanging right over our boundary fence. I've got photographs to prove it.'

`It isn't about your neighbour,' said the girl policewoman, surprisingly gently. `I'm afraid I've got some bad news for you. Could I ask if you're sitting down?'

`Of course I'm sitting down,' said Mr Caldicot, only slightly less belligerently. Mrs Caldicot could still hear his voice. `What bad news? Is it about my car? The aerial has been broken off twice this month already.'

`It isn't about your car,' said the girl policewoman, patiently. `It's about your father.'

`My father?'

`I'm afraid he's been taken ill. Very ill.'

`There must be some sort of mistake,' said Mr Caldicot. `I spoke to him last Sunday. He was perfectly healthy. Are you sure you've got the right Mr Caldicot?'

`Your mother gave us your number,' said the girl policewoman. `We're with her now.'

`At their house?'

`Yes, that's right.'

`I thought you said it was my father who'd been taken ill?'

`That's right. He's at the hospital. I'm afraid your father is dead Mr Caldicot.'

`Dead?'

`I'm afraid so. I'm very sorry to be the one to have to tell you this.'

`A moment ago you said he was very ill.'

`He's dead I'm afraid.'

`Are you sure?'

`I'm afraid so, Mr Caldicot. Would it be convenient for you to come over to stay with your mother?'

`Well it isn't really,' said Mr Caldicot. `I've got an important meeting at 3 o'clock.'

Mrs Caldicot, who had heard all this very clearly, glanced across at the policeman. He was looking at her and lowered his eyes, blushing with embarrassment.

`Your mother suggested that we rang you,' persisted the girl policewoman.

Mr Caldicot sighed deeply. `O.K.,' he said, reluctantly but resignedly abandoning himself to his fate. `I'll be over as soon as I can.'

The policewoman put the telephone down. `Your son will be here just as soon as possible,' she said. `We'll stay with you until he gets here.' She seemed unaware that Mrs Caldicot had overheard the conversation.

CHAPTER THREE

`You'll have to come and stay with us for the night!' Mr Caldicot told his mother firmly. It was much more of an order than an invitation. `Just for a night or two. Jason can sleep on the sofa.'

`I'd rather stick hot needles in my eyes,' Mrs Caldicot found herself thinking, and wondered where on earth the phrase had come from. She shivered at the thought of it. `I'll be all right,' she said politely. `I'll stay here, thank you.' She didn't like staying at her son's house. She didn't get on terribly well with Veronica, her daughter-in-law. In fact, that was something of an understatement. The truth was that she and Veronica had always rubbed each other up the wrong way, though she wasn't entirely sure why.

Veronica was a staunch Conservative party worker who dyed her hair blonde, wore pearls to breakfast and thought that a British passport still entitled you to be treated better than anyone else when coming through customs at Calais.

Mrs Caldicot didn't like her grandson very much either. Jason was sixteen, still went to bed at ten o'clock on weekdays and called his parents `Mummy' and `Daddy', apparently without any embarrassment. He collected stamps, could tell you the current bank rate and always won with ease when they played Trivial Pursuit at Christmas.

She didn't even like her son, Derek, though that wasn't anything new for even as a child she had always found him to be rather stern and humourless.

She wondered idly where all the humour had gone in her life and why no one she knew ever seemed to laugh. Her husband had never been one for laughing; he could never see the point of it. He had, she thought, probably been born pompous. He had been a qualified sanitary engineer and always took umbrage when Mrs Caldicot told people that he was in sewage. And Derek seemed physically incapable of laughter. She remembered that as a baby he didn't even laugh when you tickled him. She wondered why the ability to laugh was spread around so unevenly. Perhaps, she thought, there is only so much laughter allowed in the world and if one person has too much of it then someone else must go without. She wondered who had decided that she was to be cheated of her fair share of fun; to be sentenced to a lifetime of unrelieved solemnity.

'You can't stay here by yourself,' shouted Derek Caldicot indignantly. He was obviously repeating himself because he thought she hadn't heard him. She wished she had the nerve to tell him that nothing he ever said was worth repeating, whether anyone heard it or not. He waved a hand around. He was trying hard to remain patient. 'All this has come at a very bad time for me,' he said.

'I'm sorry,' thought Mrs Caldicot, 'that your father chose such an inconvenient time to die.' She looked at him. 'There's Kitty to look after,' she explained. 'And the chrysanthemums.' They were sitting in the kitchen and she looked out through the window at the back garden. Apart from a few square yards of lawn most of the garden was taken up with pink, blue and white chrysanthemums which had been Mr Caldicot's pride and joy. He had won prizes with his chrysanthemums.

'Damn the chrysanthemums,' said Derek. 'What do they matter now? And the neighbours will feed Kitty.'

In her heart Mrs Caldicot shared her son's none too subtly expressed feelings for her late husband's chrysanthemums. She hated them. She had always hated them. 'I must water your father's chrysanthemums,' Mrs Caldicot insisted. 'And I don't like leaving Kitty on her own at a time like this.' She looked at the cat. 'She adored your father you know,' she lied. 'She always sat on his lap of an evening.' The cat, who had hated Mr Caldicot and had never sat on his lap, pricked up her ears in anticipation and expectation each time she heard her name. Mrs Caldicot, who never normally lied, held her breath and waited for a bolt of lightning to strike her. She wondered why she had lied. She pressed both hands against her lower abdomen as though trying to squeeze away the colicky pains which gripped her.

'I can't stay with you, mother,' said Derek. He always called her mother when he thought she was behaving stupidly. 'I've got an important meeting in Wolverhampton first thing in the morning. Come on now; get your coat.' He shouted slightly when he spoke to her as though he thought she was a little deaf. Or maybe he hoped that she, like a foreigner, would be able to understand him better if he shouted. She looked at him and noticed that he had a lush growth of hair in his ears and in his nose. How could anyone take seriously someone who had hair growing out of their ears? She stared at him and wanted to giggle. `Why don't you just go away and leave me alone?' Mrs Caldicot thought.

She stood up, walked across the kitchen, opened a cupboard and took out a can of cat food. It was labelled `Turkey, Duck and Liver' and she looked at it for a moment thinking how odd the phrase looked. It sounded as though Liver were an animal. Or rather a bird. Would you, she wondered, have a flock of Livers? Maybe television programme makers would send teams off to the jungle in search of the missing liver bird. She could see David Attenborough burrowing through the bush. `And just in front of me,' he was whispering, `I can see the wild liver rampaging through the forest in search of the indigenous gin bush.' She opened the can and put several chunks of turkey, duck and liver onto a plate. She peered at the meat for a moment trying in vain to decide which meat was which. Then she put the plate down on the floor for the cat. When she had done that she opened the back door and went into the small glass-sided conservatory. She started to put on her shoes; an elderly, well-worn pair of black brogues.

`What are you doing?' Derek sounded irritable.

`I'm cleaning my teeth,' she thought. `What the devil do you think I'm doing?' She sighed. `I'm going to see your father,' she replied.

`What on earth for?'

`I want to make sure he really is dead,' thought Mrs Caldicot. `I just want to see him,' said Mrs Caldicot. She paused as she struggled with her laces. `The policeman said they'd want me to identify him,' she lied. That was the second lie she'd uttered and she realised that she had not even blushed. Maybe lying, like cooking, got easier the more you did it.

`I said I'd call in later this evening,' Derek reminded her. `I'll see to all that.'

Mrs Caldicot finished tying her laces, stood up, walked back into the kitchen and took her old brown tweed coat off a hook on the back of the door.

`If you're not coming home with me take your coat off, mother,' said Mr Caldicot firmly and loudly. He was almost shouting. `I can't bring you home if you go the hospital now. I've got to get ready to go to Wolverhampton.' He paused. `It's a very important meeting,' he added, as if repeating this would confirm its necessity.

`I'm not deaf you pompous oaf!' thought Mrs Caldicot. `I'll catch the bus home,' she said, quietly.

`You can't catch a bus!' exclaimed Mr Caldicot, as though his mother had threatened to fly home on a broomstick.

But that is exactly what she wanted to do and that is exactly what she did.

Her son drove her to the hospital where she confirmed that her husband would not be showing his chrysanthemums, eating his ham salad or going to watch any more cricket matches and then when, with a sigh, Derek said that he would drive her home Mrs Caldicot defiantly refused and insisted on walking round the corner to the bus stop.

`You can't catch a bus at this time of night!' said Derek, walking behind her, his voice heavy with exasperation.

`Why on earth not?' demanded Mrs Caldicot. `If they run buses I can catch one!' she thought. `If no one wanted me to catch one they wouldn't run them would they?'

`It isn't safe!' blustered Derek.

`What have I got to lose?' thought Mrs Caldicot who had just £3.17 in her purse and who realised with some slight surprise that she wasn't afraid. `I'll be all right, dear,' she said, soothingly.

When he had gone she wondered why she wasn't afraid and realised that you can only be afraid when you have something you're afraid of losing. Money. Possessions. Health. Life. She had nothing that she feared losing and so she wasn't afraid. She felt very liberated by this thought.

The bus came and she clambered up onto the step (her hip was playing up again and the colic was still terrible). She had a strange vision of being confronted by a highwayman dressed in a mask and brandishing a huge pair of pistols. `Your money or your life!' cried the highwayman. `You choose!' insisted Mrs Caldicot. `I really don't mind.' The highwayman, greatly bewildered by this retreated into the dark of the night and left her alone. She felt rather cheated and wondered if he'd come back but he didn't.

`Come on, love, I haven't got all night,' said the bus driver. `Where do you want to go to?' Mrs Caldicot told him her destination and offered him a note. `Haven't you got a pass?' he asked her. `No,' she said, never having acquired a bus pass because Mr Caldicot thought they reeked of charity, `I'll pay cash.'

When she got home she switched on the floodlight that lit up the back garden. Her husband had it installed so that he could work on his chrysanthemums in the evenings. She picked up the watering can and carefully soaked each of the plants, just as she had seen her husband do on so many summer evenings.

Then she collected a pair of strong scissors from the tiny greenhouse at the top of the garden. The flowers were all neatly tied to stakes and slowly, systematically and with great precision, she bent down and cut through the stem of each chrysanthemum with her scissors. And because they were all tied to stakes, none of the flowers fell over and so from a distance it was impossible to see that anything was wrong with them.

Even though it was cold, she stood on the terrace for a moment and allowed herself a little smile. She wanted the flowers to die slowly. She looked around and a weed growing through the cement between the crazy paving caught her eye. She bent towards it, instinctively reaching to pull it out. Mr Caldicot had never allowed weeds into the garden. Then she stopped herself and allowed her finger tips to just graze its leaves. She realised how strange it was that such a gentle and fragile thing could be so strong.

After she had gone indoors she made herself a cup of hot drinking chocolate and then went to bed without washing the cup or turning off the outside floodlight.

CHAPTER FOUR

When she woke up the next morning the first thing Mrs Caldicot did was to look out of the bedroom window to see how the chrysanthemums were. It was a beautiful sunny morning and she was rather surprised to see that most of the flowers still looked perfectly healthy. It was quite impossible to tell that they were all dying.

She shrugged, went downstairs, leaving the bed unmade for the first time in her adult life, and made herself a cup of strong black coffee that made her shudder when she took a sip. Then she found a large, unopened packet of best bacon in the deep freeze, took two large free range eggs from the fridge, opened a tin of tomatoes and made herself a huge fried breakfast. It was the first time she had ever cooked herself a fried breakfast. Her husband had never liked or approved of big breakfasts. He insisted it was bad for the digestion to eat so much so early in the day. Once, when the Caldicots had been on holiday in the Lake District, they had stayed at a boarding house where the landlady had offered them a cooked breakfast for an extra half a crown. Mrs Caldicot had wanted to try it but Mr Caldicot had looked down his nose at the suggestion and so they ate their usual toast and marmalade.

When she had finished the last slice of fried bread and drunk a second and then a third cup of strong black coffee, Mrs Caldicot got up from the table, deliberately wiped the crumbs from the corners of her mouth with the kitchen tea towel, slid the greasy frying pan and dirty plates into the sink and went back upstairs to get dressed. In deference to her late husband she chose a simple, dark grey dress which she had only worn twice before, a pair of black patent leather shoes and a black cardigan. She looked at herself in the mirror for a few moments before deciding that she looked far too much like a widow. She then took off the grey dress, the black cardigan and the black shoes and replaced them with a white and blue polka dot dress, a pair of white sandals and a white cardigan.

Half an hour later she caught the bus into town and got off at the stop just before the Oxfam shop where she sometimes helped out.

She walked the few yards to the charity shop in glorious summer sunshine.

'Thelma!' cried a large, shapeless woman in a heavy, pink and grey flecked suit. 'I didn't expect to see you here today.' She put her head on one side and marched towards Mrs Caldicot with her arms held out in front of her. 'How are you feeling?' she asked. A cloud of cheap and rather nasty perfume preceded the large woman and almost masked a serious case of body odour.

'I'm fine,' replied Mrs Caldicot. 'I'm on the rota,' she explained. 'I didn't want to let you down.' She backed away a few inches but failed to avoid the shapeless woman's embrace.

'Oh you silly thing!' said Mrs Leatherhead. 'It must have been a terrible shock for you,' she said. 'At the cricket match wasn't it?'

Mrs Caldicot wondered how these things got round the town so quickly. She nodded.

'Would you like a cup of coffee?'

'No, thank you,' said Mrs Caldicot, who, probably as a result of her huge breakfast had a touch of indigestion. 'What would you like me to do? Unpacking? Pricing? Shelf stocking?'

'Oh, I know,' whispered Mrs Leatherhead, conspiratorially. 'You want to keep busy! What would you prefer? I've just got a delivery of books in if you'd like to check through those. They're in the back.' She turned to serve a tall, bony woman in an ankle length garment which had lots of fringes attached to it. She was holding a shawl which she had selected from the rack by the window.

'Fine,' said Mrs Caldicot. She quite liked sorting books and there was always the added advantage that you might find something worth reading. She never felt quite so much at ease sorting second-hand clothes. She left Mrs Leatherhead and the tall bony woman haggling over the price of the shawl.

***

One and a half hours later, with the books unpacked and sorted into neat piles Mrs Caldicot put the kettle on and wandered out into the shop to tell Mrs Leatherhead that a cup of coffee was on its way.

'What are your plans now?' asked Mrs Leatherhead as they dipped their ginger nut biscuits into their drinks. 'Or is too soon for you to have thought of plans?'

`What do you mean?' asked Mrs Caldicot. `What sort of plans?'

`Oh, you know,' said Mrs Leatherhead, `are you going to sell the house and buy yourself a bungalow or are you going to move in with Derek?'

Mrs Caldicot frowned. `Why should I do either?'

`Oh you won't want to stay where you are,' said Mrs Leatherhead definitely. `Not in that big house.'

`But it isn't all that big,' protested Mrs Caldicot. `It's only got three bedrooms.'

`But, dear, all that garden! And the roof and so on. Oh you don't want that sort of responsibility on your own. Oh no! You wouldn't want to be in that house by yourself at night now, would you?'

Mrs Caldicot, who had slept in the house by herself when her husband had been away attending conferences on sewage, didn't quite know what to say to this. It had never occurred to her that she might have to move house. And why should the roof worry her, she wondered. Was someone going to steal it if she stayed there alone?

`Are you going to be all right for money?' asked Mrs Leatherhead. `Has he left you all right?'

`What business is that of yours?' thought Mrs Caldicot indignantly. Why, she wondered, did Mrs Leatherhead assume that just because she was bereaved she was also bereft of all dignity.    `I don't know,' she said. `To be honest I haven't even thought about money.'

`Oh well you must!' insisted Mrs Leatherhead. `And you watch out for solicitors and bank people and the like. My Henry says they're all crooks.'

`I wouldn't listen to anything your Henry said if my life depended on it,' thought Mrs Caldicot, nodding her head as though in acquiescence. Henry Leatherhead always claimed that he was something `rather confidential' in the civil service but in reality Mrs Caldicot knew that he worked for the Department of Employment. He was the daftest, most insipid man she had ever met. She wondered why she had allowed herself to be surrounded by such boring, inept and unattractive people. She thought gloomily of all the evenings that she and her husband had spent having dinner with the Leatherheads. It had always followed a strict ritual. Sherry. Something traditional served with gravy. Cheap wine from the supermarket. And dull conversation about the price of fish. Their evenings together had been as structured and as predictable as a church service.

'Still,' said Mrs Leatherhead. 'Whatever you do, you just take your time!' She lowered her head and popped a piece of soggy biscuit into her mouth before it could drop into the coffee beneath it. 'Whatever you decide to do you don't want to be pushed into making a decision too quickly.' She winked at Mrs Caldicot. 'You'll find yourself surrounded by people who want to give you advice,' she said. 'You ignore them all and decide for yourself exactly when you want to move and where you want to go.'

Mrs Caldicot thanked Mrs Leatherhead, but realised that she longed not for sympathy or advice but for simple encouragement. She wondered why everyone always wanted to give advice. Why, she thought, don't they offer me sympathy and support and encouragement for what I choose to do. Whatever it is. She wondered why people were so quick to offer so many answers to her problems when it was patently clear that they had little ability to deal with the problems in their own lives. Derek's life was hardly a domestic success and the Leatherheads would not have won any prizes for enviable domesticity.

'Don't mention it,' said Mrs Leatherhead, helping herself to another ginger nut from the shrinking packet. 'It's at a time like this that you really find out who your friends are. Has the doctor given you anything?'

'What do you mean?' asked Mrs Caldicot, genuinely puzzled as to why the doctor should give her anything.

'To help you sleep,' explained Mrs Leatherhead. 'For your nerves. You know.'

'Oh,' said Mrs Caldicot. 'No.'

'Well you just get yourself along there and have a word with him,' said Mrs Leatherhead firmly. 'You can never be too careful at a time like this. My friend Gladys,' she paused, 'do you know Gladys Robertson who used to be married to the butcher who had a shop in Vicarage Street behind the multi-storey car park?'

Mrs Caldicot shook her head. 'No, I don't think so.'

'He always had good tripe and our Dennis loved his sausages. Well, Gladys was as right as rain one minute, and everyone thought she was coping with it all marvellously and then suddenly, whoosh, there she was in the hospital under heavy sedation suffering from deep depression.'

'Oh,' said Mrs Caldicot.

'She tried to do away with herself,' whispered Mrs Leatherhead. 'There's only a few of us who know about it and I promised not to tell a soul but since you don't know her it doesn't really count, does it?'

'It depends how seriously you take a promise,' thought Mrs Caldicot. 'No, I suppose not,' she agreed.

'She was on tablets for months and months and they gave her that electrical treatment where they connect your brain up to the mains and give it an electric shock to shake it back into sense, you know.'

'No, I haven't heard of that,' said Mrs Caldicot, shivering a little with distaste and hoping that her own strange compunctions weren't anything very much to worry about. She suddenly remembered the chrysanthemums and hoped that no one would regard that as a sign of madness, though she did think that perhaps she could claim it was the work of vandals if she said she'd heard a noise at night.

'I think I heard people in the garden last night,' she said suddenly.

'Good heavens!' said Mrs Leatherhead. 'There you are, you see! They've got no scruples these days, burglars. They hear of a man dying and a woman in the house by herself and they're round there straight away.' She shivered noticeably and a small cloud of face powder floated through a bright beam of sunshine. 'The quicker you're out of that place the better. You want to get someone round to have a look at the property for you.' She stopped and snorted. 'But then, what am I saying,' she carried on, 'you've got your Derek haven't you? In the business and everything.'

'I think it was probably just vandals,' said Mrs Caldicot quickly, immediately regretting the untruth. 'Children I expect. In the garden.'

'At least that'll save you a few pounds on estate agency fees,' said Mrs Leatherhead. 'Your Derek will be able to get it all done for you free won't he?'

'All what?' asked Mrs Caldicot.

'You know, the estate agency stuff; the boards and the advertising and the solicitors and so on.'

'I don't know. Possibly.'

'There you are then,' said Mrs Leatherhead. 'That's often the worst of it all. With your Derek to look after things you'll be very well placed.'

`Not the solicitors though I don't expect.' said Mrs Caldicot.

Just then a customer came over wanting to know if the hand carved wooden ashtrays would mark if you left a cigarette end burning in them and Mrs Caldicot took the opportunity to wave goodbye to Mrs Leatherhead and to slip out into the street.

When she got back home the chrysanthemums were looking decidedly glum. Petals were going brown and starting to fall off all over the garden. Mrs Caldicot stared out at them and wondered why she'd bothered. Just then the telephone rang.

`It's Victor,' said a voice she recognised at once. Victor Reynolds. Another keen gardener. Friend of her late husband and long time chrysanthemum grower. `I was very sorry to hear about George.'

`Yes,' said Mrs Caldicot. `Thank you.'

`I was just thinking,' said Victor. `Would you like me to show his chrysanthemums for him? In his name, of course.'

Mrs Caldicot stared out of the window at the drooping flowers and falling petals.

`It seemed a pity not to,' said Victor. `I thought it might be a gesture he would appreciate.'

`I'm afraid it's too late,' said Mrs Caldicot. `The vandals have got at them.'

`The vandals? What do you mean?'

`They've cut the stems,' said Mrs Caldicot. `They're all dying.'

`Oh dear me. Oh dear oh dear,' said Victor. `Oh, that's terrible.' He sounded quite distraught.

`Yes,' said Mrs Caldicot. `It's awful what they'll do, isn't it?'

`I don't know what to say,' said Victor. `I'm speechless.'

`No, you're not,' thought Mrs Caldicot. `You're wittering on and you're making far more fuss over the damned chrysanthemums than you did over George.' `Yes,' she said.

`Well, then,' said Victor. `I don't suppose there's anything to be done.'

`No.' said Mrs Caldicot. `I don't suppose so.'

`Goodbye then,' said Victor. And she heard the receiver go down and the next moment the telephone went dead. She put the receiver down and stared at the dying chrysanthemums, silently hoping that they were suffering.

CHAPTER FIVE

Mrs Caldicot looked out of the bedroom window on the second full day of her bereavement and stared at the garden. `My second day of living,' she thought. The chrysanthemums were mostly dead now. She smiled at them with quiet delight then slipped into her comfortable, candlewick dressing gown and headed for the stairs.

As she tied her dressing gown belt firmly around her waist she thought how much she hated the garment. Come to that she hated most of her clothes. In or out of the house she had invariably dressed to please her late husband. For the last thirty years of her life she hadn't ever thought about what *she* wanted to wear when she had been choosing clothes. She had automatically bought what she knew *he* would expect her to wear. Some men wanted their wives to wear clinging, feminine garments made of silk; more frilly and chilly than hard-wearing or warm. But Mr Caldicot had favoured sensible, long-lasting suits; sensible shoes and sensible nightwear. Nothing fashionable. Nothing flimsy. Nothing colourful. Nothing frivolous. He had believed that clothes should be functional, hard-wearing and inexpensive. She made a silent vow to go into the shops to buy herself something different.

The telephone began to ring and she hurried to the kitchen to pick it up. `I thought you'd gone out!' complained her son Derek. `Where were you?'

`Drunk in bed after last night's party,' thought Mrs Caldicot. She laughed out loud and then realised with horror that she had nearly said what she had thought.

`What's the matter?' asked Derek, who must have heard the laugh.

`Nothing,' said Mrs Caldicot, quickly. She couldn't remember the last time she had laughed. She felt that she was blushing. She picked up her handbag, which was still standing where she had left it on the kitchen table, opened it and took out her make-up mirror. She peeped into it. Her cheeks were bright red. These secret thoughts seemed to be coming thicker and faster than ever now that she was on her own.

`Did you hear me?' demanded Derek, crossly.

`No. Sorry. I wasn't concentrating.' said Mrs Caldicot.

`I don't know what's the matter with you,' sighed Derek. He sounded exasperated. `You've been acting very strangely.'

`You haven't seen anything yet!' thought Mrs Caldicot. `Your father's just died,' she said.

`That's what I was ringing about,' said Derek. `I've arranged the funeral for the day after tomorrow. They can't do it any sooner because there's got to be an autopsy.'

`I thought you were going to Wolverhampton,' said Mrs Caldicot.

`I am in Wolverhampton,' said Derek.

`What on earth did you want to go to Wolverhampton for?' asked Mrs Caldicot. `Why would anyone want to go to Wolverhampton?' she thought.

`I didn't have any choice in the matter,' said Derek wearily. `I told you before – I have a very important meeting with a possible client. I'm coming back tonight. Now are you sure that you're all right?'

`Is it a good meeting?' asked Mrs Caldicot. She wondered why meetings and conferences were always very important. Didn't anyone ever hold meetings and conferences that were just ordinarily important? Her late husband's numerous meetings and conferences had always been described as very important and she'd never understood how so many men in sewage could think of so many reasons for having very important conferences. What, she wondered, did they find to talk about? How did they manage to make such a simple business so complicated? Why did they need to hold week long conferences in Margate to discuss sewage?

Derek was talking. She decided she ought to concentrate. `...thank you. If you're not alright I'll get Veronica to come round and sit with you for a few hours.'

`Oh no! Not Veronica! I'll do anything if you keep Veronica away from me!' thought Mrs Caldicot. `I'm fine, thank you,' she said.

`I've arranged for a cremation not a burial. You don't object do you?'

`I don't mind whether they burn him, bury him or leave him out with the rubbish,' she thought. `No.' she said.

`When I get back I want to talk to you about selling the house,' said Derek. `It isn't a good time to sell but you can't stay there by yourself. I've made an appointment for you to see your solicitor at 2.30 this afternoon. He needs to talk to you about the will.'

`I don't want to sell the house!' said Mrs Caldicot. Then she wondered why she had said that. Maybe selling was the right thing to do. She didn't much like the house. She never had. Come to think of it she hated the house, the furniture and the chrysanthemums. Maybe she would, after all, let him persuade her to sell it. Maybe.

`Please, don't be so difficult all the time, mother,' sighed Derek. `I've got to go now. We'll talk about it when I get back. Did you hear what I said about the solicitor?'

`Yes. Two thirty this afternoon. I didn't know we had a solicitor.'

`He does a lot of work with us,' said Derek. `And he drew up Dad's will a few years ago.'

`Oh.' said Mrs Caldicot. She hadn't thought about a will. She hadn't even known that there was a will.

`I'll ring you tonight,' said Derek. `O.K.?'

`Yes. Bye then,' said Mrs Caldicot. `Oh, Derek!' she said, quickly, before he could put the phone down.

`Yes?'

`Have you got a clean vest on?'

There was a sigh. `Yes, mother.'

`And a clean handkerchief?'

Another sigh. `Yes, mother.'

`Good boy.' said Mrs Caldicot. She had to bite her cheek to stop herself from laughing out loud. `And don't forget to thank those nice people in Wolverhampton for having you before you come home,' she added, but it was too late for Derek had put his receiver down and broken the connection.

Mrs Caldicot cooked herself some breakfast, added the dirty dishes to the growing pile in the sink and got dressed. Then she headed into town to do some serious shopping.

***

`What about this one, madam?' asked the sales assistant, approaching Mrs Caldicot and offering her a woollen suit in a particularly nauseating shade of camouflage green. The assistant, who looked as though she nurtured an aching longing to be in her late twenties, had heavy false eyelashes, scarlet lips and bright red finger nails. She was not in her late twenties and had not been in her late twenties for a generation or so. She wore a grey suit with a skirt that ended a good three inches above her knees and she arrived in a cloud of suffocating scent. She had a badge on her left lapel which gave her name as `Daphne' and her designation as `Senior Sales Assistant'. She had an unlikely chest which cocked a snook at gravity, and which Mrs Caldicot suspected probably relied heavily on more hidden structural engineering work than the average suspension bridge.

Mrs Caldicot looked at the woollen suit with distaste. `I'm looking for something a little less stern,' she explained. She looked down at her own olive skirt and jumper. `I don't usually dress like this,' she lied, suspecting that the assistant was trying to find her something which matched the style she was wearing. `I had to borrow these from a friend,' she lied. `All my own clothes were destroyed in a fire.' Lying *was* like cooking. It did get easier the more you did it.

`Perhaps madam would give me an idea of the sort of direction in which I should be looking,' said the assistant.

`Those over there look rather nice,' said Mrs Caldicot, picking out a row of scoop necked summer dresses in pastel colours. `Pink. I think I might like pink.'

The assistant, trying unsuccessfully to disguise her look of surprise, swished across to the rail and flicked through the dresses quickly; sending the hangers whizzing along the chromium plated rail with experienced ease. `These do have the zip up the back,' she warned, plucking a pale pink dress from the rail and holding it out so that Mrs Caldicot could examine it.

`I don't mind where the zip is,' said Mrs Caldicot.

`Some of our more mature customers dislike back fastening,' confided Daphne. `Arthritis and so on, you know,' she confided.

`That must be terrible,' agreed Mrs Caldicot. She toyed with the zip. `This is a little, well, functional, isn't it?' she smiled. `Do you have anything a little more frivolous?'

`Frivolous, madam?'

`Yes,' said Mrs Caldicot firmly. `Frivolous. Buttons, maybe. Lots and lots of very tiny buttons.' She took the dress and held it up against her. `And I'd like something with less sleeve and more of a plunge at the front. I'd like to show a little...'she blushed. `You know...'

`Cleavage, madam?'

`Exactly!' said Mrs Caldicot. `Yes. That's the word. Cleavage.'
She said it defiantly. `I'd like to show a little cleavage.'

`Certainly, madam!' said Daphne. The sales assistant smiled
conspiratorially. `May I ask, madam, is this for a special occasion?'

`Yes,' said Mrs Caldicot, wickedly. `A funeral. My husband's
funeral.'

***

She wore her new dress to visit the solicitor.

`Your husband left a few small bequests but basically the bulk of
his estate goes to you,' said Mr Suffolk. He was a breezy, cheerful
sort of fellow who seemed to be in rather a hurry. He wore a light
grey polyester suit, a white nylon shirt and a plain red polyester tie.
`I must say your husband was an extraordinarily efficient and well
organised man.'

Mrs Caldicot smiled politely at this compliment, although she
would have preferred to describe her husband as obsessional and nit-
picking. Every month he had insisted on going through the
household expenses with her.

`You've spent £1.18 more on coffee this month,' he would say,
pointing a podgy finger at the appropriate figures.

`That's because the supermarket prices sometimes vary,' Mrs
Caldicot would reply. `Or because we've drunk more coffee this
month.'

`And why did you spend 68 pence more on toilet rolls?' he would
demand.

`You had diarrhoea for two days after you came back from that
conference in Brighton,' she would answer.

`Normally,' continued the solicitor, `it takes a few weeks to work
out the size of an estate but in your case I can tell you now that your
husband has left you quite well off.'

Mrs Caldicot frowned. `Just what does `quite well off' mean?'

`It means that you won't have to worry too much about where
your next meal is going to come from,' said Mr Suffolk, with a
`Don't you worry your head about the figures' smile. `Your husband
was a cautious man who preferred to put most of his money into the
building society rather than to invest it on the stock market, and the
last few years have justified his caution.'

`That's nice,' said Mrs Caldicot.

`There's certainly enough to merit professional management,' said the solicitor.

`Aha! Here it comes,' thought Mrs Caldicot.

`Our firm specialises in estate management and we would be very happy to manage your money for you.'

`I'll bet you would,' thought Mrs Caldicot. `That's very kind of you,' she said. `But I'd like to take a little time to think things over first.' She had never noticed herself being so cynical before. `If the building society did well for my husband maybe I'll just leave it there for the time being.'

`Well, the building society isn't always the best answer,' said the solicitor, rather hurriedly. `And I couldn't take responsibility for your continued financial health were you to decide to leave your estate in the building society indefinitely.'

`Nevertheless, I'd like to think about things,' said Mrs Caldicot.

`Of course,' smiled the solicitor, somehow managing to sound patronising while saying only two words.

CHAPTER SIX

Mrs Caldicot had just got out of the bath and, dressed in a new, shocking pink nightdress and a new bright pink satin dressing gown had gone down to the living room to watch television with a plate of egg and tomato sandwiches resting on one arm of her favourite armchair and a large glass of red wine perched precariously on the other when the front door bell rang. Muttering quiet curses to no one in particular Mrs Caldicot lifted Kitty from her lap and answered the door.

`Good evening, mother,' said Derek, pecking her on the cheek and walking past her into the hallway.

`Good evening, mother,' said Veronica, his wife, brushing her lips through the air close to Mrs Caldicot's cheek and following him into the hall. She wore a pleated navy blue skirt and a lime green blouse and carried a potted geranium in her hands.

Jason, their son mumbled something which could have been `Good evening, grandma.' As he reached out with pursed lips Mrs Caldicot swayed skilfully out of reach and noticed with satisfaction that his spots were redder and more pustulant than ever. He wore a pair of headphones connected to a small box which was attached to his belt, and a continuous and annoying tinny noise escaped from the headphones. She could not remember ever seeing him without this piece of equipment.

`Good evening,' said Mrs Caldicot, shutting the front door behind them. `Do come in.' Her intestines began to tighten up in anticipation. Her tummy pains, which were always bad when she saw Derek, were always far worse when she saw Veronica as well.

`We thought we'd come round and see how you're bearing up,' said Derek.

`I've brought you a geranium,' said Veronica. She held the plant out so that Mrs Caldicot could inspect it.

`So you did!' said Mrs Caldicot. `What a nice pot.' She hated geraniums almost as much as she hated chrysanthemums. She went back into the living room but did not take the offered gift from her daughter-in-law and so Veronica was left holding the plant. The three visitors followed Mrs Caldicot. Jason sat down on the sofa, pulled a book of chess problems out of his pocket and started to read.

`I was just having a bite to eat,' said Mrs Caldicot. She saw Derek and Veronica exchange glances. `I just fancied a sandwich in front of the television,' she explained unnecessarily. She had been quite looking forward to a quiet evening on her own.

`And a glass of wine, I see!' said Derek. There was more than a hint of disapproval in his voice.

`Yes,' agreed Mrs Caldicot. `And a glass of wine.'

`It's a little early to be drinking isn't it, mother?'

Mrs Caldicot looked at the clock. It was half past seven. She couldn't think of any suitable retort so she kept silent.

`And alone, too!' added Derek sternly.

`If there had been anyone else here I would have offered them a drink,' thought Mrs Caldicot. She smiled brightly. `You're here now! Would you like a drink?'

`No thank you, mother!' said Derek. `I'm driving.'

Mrs Caldicot turned to offer her daughter-in-law a drink but Veronica had put the potted plant down on the sideboard, and was looking out of the window at the back garden. `Good heavens!' She exclaimed suddenly. `Derek! Just come and look at this!'

Derek obeyed and together the two of them stared out at the crop of dead chrysanthemums. Because they were all firmly tied to canes the flowers, though dead, were still standing erect.

`What on earth has happened?' asked Veronica. `They look as if they're all dead!'

`I thought you said you were going to water them!' said Derek to his mother.

`I did,' said Mrs Caldicot. `But someone cut through all the stems!'

`Oh that's terrible!' cried Veronica. Why, Mrs Caldicot wondered, did so many people care so much about a garden full of chrysanthemums. They would have died soon anyway.

`Well that settles it,' said Derek. `You can't stay here.' He opened the French doors and stepped out onto the patio.

Mrs Caldicot frowned. `Why? Because the chrysanthemums are dead?' She moved to the doorway and looked around. `But I didn't like them anyway.'

`No,' said Derek patiently. He was getting worried about his mother who seemed either to be changing personality or developing a sense of humour. He wasn't sure which, but found both possibilities equally daunting. `Not because the chrysanthemums are dead but because someone killed them.' He stressed the words `someone', `dead' and `killed' and made the demise of the chrysanthemums sound like mass murder. He bent down and examined the stems of the flowers nearest to the back door, then turned his head and looked back at her. `These have all been cut through,' he announced. `Probably with a sharp knife or a pair of scissors,' he added. Derek, who was not a fit man, stood up and rubbed the small of his back as though he'd been gardening for hours. `Have you called the police?'

Mrs Caldicot frowned. `No.'

`You should have done,' said Derek.

`But what on earth could they do?'

`Fingerprints!' said Derek. He looked around. `Footprints, possibly.' He stared sternly at a small plastic gnome which was sitting on a red and white spotted mushroom. `If only he could talk,' he said. `I bet he could tell us a thing or two.'

`He's loyal. He wouldn't talk,' thought Mrs Caldicot.

`I suspect the police have got more important things to do than worry about a few dead chrysanthemums,' she said. She had a vision of squads of policemen racing around the countryside looking for the Phantom Chrysanth Killer. `What are you looking for?' she called as Derek wandered off peering down among the chrysanthemums.

`The knife they used!' said Derek. `They may have thrown it down somewhere.'

`Oh I wouldn't have thought so,' said Mrs Caldicot, moving back indoors.

`We'll get you into a home where you'll be safe,' said Veronica who had sat herself down next to her son. She looked across at Mrs Caldicot's plate of egg and tomato sandwiches. `And they'll make sure that you eat properly.' She wagged a finger and a pair of heavy false eyelashes. `You need regular hot meals inside you!'

`Would you like one?' asked Mrs Caldicot, ignoring the advice, picking up the plate and offering her daughter-in-law a sandwich.

`Oh, no thank you,' said Veronica, holding up a hand in horror. `I'm on a diet.'

`It doesn't show,' thought Mrs Caldicot. `That's nice,' she said, smiling sweetly.

Derek came back into the living room, closed the French doors behind him, making sure that they were firmly locked. His muddy shoes left grubby footprints on the carpet. `Just make sure you check all the windows before you go to bed tonight,' he told Mrs Caldicot. `Whoever did this may come back,' he warned her gloomily.

`What would you say if I told you that the person who did this would be in my bedroom all night,' thought Mrs Caldicot. `I don't think so,' she said. `I haven't got any more chrysanthemums.' She smiled weakly and sat down. Kitty jumped onto her lap and Mrs Caldicot tickled her under the chin. `I wish I had someone to tickle me under the chin,' thought Mrs Caldicot. She stopped tickling the cat and tried it on herself. It felt rather nice.

`What on earth are you doing, mother?' asked Derek.

`I had an itch,' said Mrs Caldicot. `Probably a flea,' she smiled. `You know what cats are like.'

Veronica winced noticeably.

`I've tried to stop her climbing onto the furniture,' said Mrs Caldicot. `But it's impossible. She gets everywhere.'

Veronica pulled her skirt down to cover as much of her legs as possible and then stood up. `We must be going,' she said. `We just wanted to see that you were all right.'

She and Derek headed for the door.

`We'll pick you up in the morning for the funeral,' said Derek, whispering the final word.

`Come along, Jason, dear,' said Veronica.

`Yes, mummy,' said Jason. He carefully put a slip of paper into the page he had been reading and put the book into his pocket and stood up.

`Goodbye,' called Mrs Caldicot as her uninvited visitors trooped out through the front door.

`Goodbye, mother!' said Derek.

`Goodbye, mother!' said Veronica.

`Goodbye, grandma!' said Jason.

`Thank you for the geranium,' said Mrs Caldicot.

She went back into the living room, switched on the television, picked up an egg and tomato sandwich, took a large bite and then started to tickle herself under her chin with her free hand.

CHAPTER SEVEN

It had not, thought Mrs Caldicot, been a very impressive turn out. Her husband, who always tended to judge people by appearances, would have been mortified if he had been there to see it.

`Father would have been pleased,' claimed Derek, who had inherited his understanding of people from Mr Caldicot. `Quite a good turn out.'

`If he'd been here he would have been glad he was dead,' thought Mrs Caldicot ruefully.

The fire and brimstone stuff was over and they had returned to Derek's spacious, detached, architect-designed house for what Mrs Caldicot secretly thought of as `the essential post burn up beano'. Derek's home, which had four bedrooms, two reception rooms, a garage for two cars, a large garden and a large kitchen with built in oven, microwave and dishwasher, was conveniently situated for local schools and shops in a pleasant suburban area. Mrs Caldicot looked around at the other mourners. There weren't many of them, despite the attractions of a free lunch.

Apart from Derek (dressed in a black morning suit and his Estate Agents Association tie), Veronica (dressed in a black chiffon dress and still carrying a black parasol hooked over her arm) and Jason (wearing an ill-fitting electric blue suit, the inescapable headphones and two tubes of acne cream and sitting hunched over an electronic pocket chess set) there were just five other mourners; Mr and Mrs Leatherhead; two men from the Sewage Works who Mrs Caldicot vaguely recognised (she would have known where they were from even if she had not recognised them for they both brought with them the curiously sweet smell that her late husband had brought home with him every evening for thirty years) and a man whose name she had forgotten but who had introduced himself as representing the Chrysanthemum Society and who had brought with him a sturdy looking wreath made entirely out of chrysanthemums.

However many times you added them up it could not, she thought, be described as a `good turnout'. She had worried for several minutes over the fact that Derek was wearing a morning suit and had eventually come to the conclusion that he had hired it in error, assuming that the ensemble was a `mourning suit'. It was an error that delighted her in some strange way, though the delight was constrained by the fact that she did not feel able to share this discovery with any of the other guests.

Now that the funeral itself was over she felt glad that she hadn't put on her new pink dress but had instead chosen to wear a dark grey tweed suit that she had bought and worn for her own mother's funeral some years earlier. Not even Mr Caldicot, deprived of a proper mourning, deserved that much humiliation.

Mrs Caldicot, suddenly aware that someone standing beside her had spoken to her, turned and found Veronica hovering by her elbow. `I beg your pardon?'

`I said would you like another sausage roll?'

Veronica, who had now added a quilted oven glove in blue and green to her funereal ensemble, was holding a glass plate upon which half a dozen sausage rolls were reclining on a white paper napkin. The paper napkin had small green holly leaves and tiny red berries printed in a neat pattern around its edge. `Be careful!' she warned. `They're hot!' She had lipstick on her teeth and flakes of pastry at the corner of her mouth showed that she had at least had the guts to eat her own produce.

`Thank you, no,' said Mrs Caldicot, `I've had one already.' She smiled and held up a hand like a policeman on traffic duty. `I'd like to live long enough to enjoy some of the money I've been left,' she thought. Veronica was not a woman to whom cooking came easily, and Mrs Caldicot knew from past experience that if there was a word which most accurately summed up the consequences of Veronica's culinary skills it was probably `indigestion'. Most of the remaining sausage rolls were so black that Mrs Caldicot couldn't help thinking that they were exceptionally suitable for a post-crematorium feast.

Mrs Caldicot hadn't wanted a reception after the cremation but Derek had insisted that you couldn't expect people to turn out to a funeral unless you gave them something to eat and drink afterwards. Mrs Caldicot wondered if Derek might not have been the first person to coin the concept that there is no such thing as a free mourner.

`I think you're being very brave,' said Veronica, resting her free hand on Mrs Caldicot's forearm. `Very brave, indeed.'

`Thank you,' said Mrs Caldicot gracefully.

`Derek and I have found a lovely home for you,' smiled Veronica. `You'll be very happy there.'

Mrs Caldicot was rather taken aback at this. She had not expected her son to have moved quite so speedily. She winced as the pains in her intestine suddenly grew stronger.

`We'll take you there when everyone's gone,' promised Veronica. `Just to have a look around.' She patted Mrs Caldicot on the arm. `They've got fitted carpets, colour television and running water in all the rooms,' she whispered, just before she drifted away to offer her incinerated sausage rolls to the two sewage workers.

Mrs Caldicot felt very glum. She didn't feel old enough to be put into a home, even if the floors were carpeted. The death of her husband had left her aware that she had wasted most of her life on doing the laundry for a man whose main ambition had been to make sure that he got an annual parking space at the Mettleham Cricket Ground. `I wouldn't have minded being behind a man who stood for something,' she thought. Years of frustration had bubbled to the surface and, released at last by Mr Caldicot's unexpected demise, were now threatening to soar out of control. She sat gloomily in a corner contemplating a future spent in a carpeted ante-room to death, waiting for her allotted place on the conveyor belt in the crematorium.

`They're all going now, mother,' murmured Derek a little while later.

Mrs Caldicot looked up and realised how much she hated being called `mother' and wondered why a few brief moments of clumsy and unsatisfying coupling, followed nine months later by several hours of painful and unrewarding parturition had been allowed to dominate her life ever afterwards. Mr and Mrs Leatherhead, the man from the Chrysanthemum Society and the two sewage engineers were all crowding into the doorway on the other side of the room and waving diffident goodbyes. The two sewage engineers, she noticed, both carried something wrapped in white paper napkins. Mrs Caldicot raised a hand and waved to them as they filed out of the living room and headed back towards reality.

`What were the two sewage engineers carrying?' she asked Veronica when they had all gone.

`I gave them a couple of spare sausage rolls each,' explained Veronica with a proud look on her face. `They liked them so much.'

`Come on now, mother,' said Derek, `shall we take you round to see your new home?'

***

According to the brochure which Veronica gave Mrs Caldicot to read in the car `The Twilight Years Rest Home stood in three-quarters of an acre of gently rolling parkland' and provided `a combination of the traditional and the modern'. An artist's colourful impression of one of the bedrooms showed magnificent antique furniture and a discreetly positioned electrocardiogram monitor.

What the brochure didn't explain, and what no one had troubled to tell the artist, was that the word `traditional' referred to the medical equipment and the word `modern' referred to the furniture. The proprietors of The Twilight Years Rest Home had also overlooked the fact that when you tarmacadam a large area for a car park there isn't much left out of three-quarters of an acre of rolling parkland.

The proprietor, Mr Fuller-Hawksmoor, was busy serving lunch when Derek, Veronica, Jason and Mrs Caldicot trooped up to the front door to inspect the home, and this meant that the normally pungent olfactory consequence of incontinence had been temporarily overwhelmed by the slightly less offensive smell of cooked cabbage.

`Yes?' snapped a dapper, little fellow wearing a light brown toupee, responding to Derek's fourth and most prolonged use of the doorbell. `It's lunchtime. We don't allow visitors at lunchtime.'

`The name's Caldicot,' explained Derek quickly but diffidently. `I've brought my mother to have a look around...'

`What a nice smell of cooking!' said Veronica. `It's cabbage isn't it?'

`Fuller-Hawksmoor,' said the small man, introducing himself, replacing his scowl with a smile and opening the front door wide so that Derek, Veronica, Jason and Mrs Caldicot could enter. He nodded to each Caldicot as they passed over the threshold, and only Mrs Caldicot noticed him check his toupee in the gilt-framed mirror on the other side of the halfway. He wore a dark suit with a grey cardigan underneath it and had, thought Mrs Caldicot, an unpleasant, rather arrogant air about him. She instinctively disliked him.

`Do you like cabbage?' he asked Veronica as she passed him.

`Oh, it's my absolute favourite!' she enthused. `It's such a nutritious vegetable.'

'Especially when it's over cooked,' thought Mrs Caldicot.

'I'm afraid we're serving luncheon at the moment,' apologised Mr Fuller-Hawksmoor quite unnecessarily. He turned to Mrs Caldicot. 'We pride ourselves on our high culinary standards,' he told her confidentially. 'Today our residents are being served with Argentinean beef substitute croquettes, pommes frites and parsnips with a choice of sea salt or black pepper topping and the green vegetable of the day, of course.'

'That's the cabbage,' suggested Mrs Caldicot.

'Absolutely!' agreed Mr Fuller-Hawksmoor. 'We like to give our residents plenty of cabbage. It's so rich in iron and other essential minerals.'

'Not when your cook has finished with it,' thought Mrs Caldicot. 'How nice,' she said, wondering why her son hated her so much that he wanted to dump her with Mr Fuller-Hawksmoor.

'Would you like to see one of the bedrooms?' Mr Fuller-Hawksmoor asked.

'That would be nice, wouldn't it, mother?' said Derek.

'Lovely,' said Mrs Caldicot.

She moved a few inches closer to her son. 'Is this a hospital?' she asked him.

'Of course it isn't!' he whispered back. 'It's a rest home. More of a hotel really.'

Mr Fuller-Hawksmoor led the way upstairs and as she followed behind him and the rest of her family, Mrs Caldicot caught a glimpse, through a half open doorway, of the dining room. A dozen or more residents were sitting on green, wipe clean plastic chairs which were arranged around a few matching green formica-topped, metal-legged tables. There were no tablecloths, and the subdued sounds of knives and forks on plates suggested that the cutlery was made of plastic. On the other side of the hallway Mrs Caldicot had a glimpse of a sitting room. Once again the chairs were covered in plastic, but this time the plastic was red rather than green.

'We have a wonderful atmosphere here,' called Mr Fuller-Hawksmoor over his shoulder. 'Every Christmas we have a party for all the residents. Last year we had a magician and the year before we had a real clown who used to be in the circus.'

'I'm glad the clown was real,' thought Mrs Caldicot facetiously. 'I hate fake clowns.'

`How many bedrooms do you have?' asked Derek.

`Seven,' answered Mr Fuller-Hawksmoor. `Four trebles and three doubles.'

`You don't have any singles?' asked Derek.

`We like to encourage our residents to think of this as their home,' said Mr Fuller-Hawksmoor. `Sharing a room with another resident helps to cement that feeling.' He stopped outside a white painted door upon which there was a small plastic plaque describing the area on the other side of the door as The Windsor Suite.

`We have a vacancy in here,' said Mr Fuller-Hawksmoor, standing aside to let the Caldicot inspection party through. There were three single divan beds in the room, which also contained a small television set on a metal trolley, two wardrobes and a sink. The floor was covered with material which an imaginative and forceful carpet salesman would have probably described as `serviceable'. One of the beds was occupied by an elderly, grey-haired, grey-faced woman who seemed to be in some distress. When she saw Mr Fuller-Hawksmoor she wearily raised a hand from the bed. `Have you brought my bedpan?' she asked timidly.

`In a moment, Miss Nightingale,' said Mr Fuller-Hawksmoor, rather crossly. `Nurse Peters will bring you a bedpan the moment she has finished serving the luncheons.' He turned to Derek with an ingratiating smile on his face. `Some of the older residents do become a little self-centred from time to time,' he said apologetically. `We find we have to be firm to be kind.'

`How many nurses do you have?' asked Veronica.

`Five,' said Mr Fuller-Hawksmoor. `All part time, but fully trained auxiliaries, of course. Two of them have certificates in first aid and Miss Pilton has just completed a local technical college course in Hairdressing and Practical Beauty with distinction.'

`That's very impressive!' said Veronica. Mrs Caldicot stared at her in disbelief.

`We pride ourselves on running a home that has all the advantages of a hotel and a fully equipped hospital,' said Mr Fuller-Hawksmoor. `Employing fully trained staff is a vital way of implementing that policy.'

Jason switched on the television set and an assortment of diagonal black and white lines flickered up and down the screen.

`Jason!' hissed Veronica. `Switch it off!'

Jason obediently switched the television set off.

`I believe the set in this suite does have some minor fault at the moment,' explained Mr Fuller-Hawksmoor, apologetically, `but there is, of course, a fully operational set of audiovisual equipment in the Duke of Devonshire Leisure and Recreational Area.'

`Do you have a video recorder?' asked Derek.

`Indeed, we do!' said Mr Fuller-Hawksmoor with pride. `I can't show it to you at the moment as it is currently receiving servicing attention, but our engineers assure us that it will back in the Recreational Area in a very short space of time.'

`Splendid,' said Derek. `There you are, mother!' he said. `You'll be able to rent video films and show them to your friends.'

``The Texas Chain Saw Massacre' might be a good starting point,' thought Mrs Caldicot, who had never rented a video film in her life. `What a lovely thought,' she said.

Mr Fuller-Hawksmoor led the way back downstairs.

`Do you have any other questions?' he asked them.

`No, I don't think so, thank you!' said Derek. `We've been very impressed, haven't we?' He looked around him as he spoke.

`Very impressed,' agreed Veronica.

`I'll give you a telephone call within the next 24 hours to let you know when my mother will be ready to move in,' said Derek.

`Wonderful!' said Mr Fuller-Hawksmoor, stopping himself from rubbing his hands together just in time. He looked at Mrs Caldicot and smiled. `We look forward to welcoming you as one of the family.'

`If your family is anything like mine that will be a real joy,' thought Mrs Caldicot. `I don't want to hold you up,' she said. `I'm sure you'll want to rush off and arrange for that poor lady upstairs to get her bed pan.'

`Exactly!' said Mr Fuller-Hawksmoor. `You're very kind.' He leant towards Derek. `It's always a privilege to have a member of such a significant local family in our establishment,' he murmured.

And with that the Caldicots trooped out through the hall, down the long stone staircase at the front of the house and back out into the real world.

`I just know you're going to be so happy there,' said Derek, puffed up with Mr Fuller-Hawksmoor's flattery, as they drove out through the grandiose iron gates which marked the entrance to the rest home and headed back to the house that Mrs Caldicot had called home for most of her life. `I don't mind admitting that I think we got rather special treatment there.' He took a hand off the steering wheel and patted his hair. `I rather suspect that he knows who I am,' he murmured.

Mrs Caldicot, enveloped in what she feared might be the beginnings of a deep depression, did not reply.

CHAPTER EIGHT

Mrs Caldicot sat staring glumly out of the living room window. Outside in the garden Derek was struggling to collect together the short canes which had previously supported the now very dead chrysanthemums. `These are very expensive to buy,' he'd told Mrs Caldicot. `I'll bundle them up and put them in the potting shed.' It had been overcast and cloudy when Derek had started. Now it was raining heavily and Derek had wrapped an old coat around his shoulders. Mrs Caldicot assumed that he had found the old coat in the potting shed for she did not recognise it. Each cane was tied in two places to the flower it had supported and Derek, who didn't realise that the short pieces of orange plastic baler twine which Mr Caldicot had used to tie up his plants were designed to be untied and used again, was struggling to cut through the ties with his tiny pocket knife. Dead flowers littered the garden where, bereft of their supporting stakes, they had fallen to the ground. On the sofa opposite Mrs Caldicot her grandson Jason, absent from school for some unexplained reason, was listening to his usual tinny noise and studying a book about nuclear physics which he seemed to be enjoying. In the hallway Veronica, who had gone to answer the door, was talking to someone whose voice Mrs Caldicot did not immediately recognise.

`Look who's come to see you!' cried Veronica, feigning surprise without real effort or conviction. `It's the doctor!' she announced, as though a travelling physician had for some reason arrived entirely unexpectedly and without invitation. Veronica had dressed for this occasion in a maroon skirt and yellow jumper, bravely ignoring the fact that neither of these colours sat comfortably with her hair which seemed a slightly lighter shade of blonde than usual. She wore her best imitation pearls, had complicated looking marcasite earrings dangling from her earlobes and tottered on shoes which had slightly higher heels than were comfortable.

The doctor, apparently unembarrassed by the mild deceit of Veronica's introduction, strode into the room with his shiny, black leather bag in one hand and a prescription pad at the ready in the other. `Good morning!' he cried with false bonhomie. `I was passing and so I thought I'd pop in and see how we were doing!' The lie slipped from lips with such self-assurance and practised ease that Mrs Caldicot wondered if he even knew that it was a lie. She found herself wondering if doctors were taught how to lie at medical school, or if medical schools deliberately selected students who were good at telling fibs. He put his bag down on the floor and stared down at her.

`You seem to be doing all right,' thought Mrs Caldicot in response to the doctor's introductory comment. `Nice suit. Expensive tie. And those shoes weren't cheap.' She stared at the doctor. Although she felt sure that she didn't really know him she nevertheless thought that she vaguely recognised him, and she tried hard to remember when and where she had seen him last.

`Your daughter-in-law tells me that you've been a bit down in the dumps since your husband passed away,' said the doctor, abandoning without embarrassment the fiction of his accidental arrival. `Not surprising, of course,' he added, exhibiting a previously unexposed strain of understanding.

Mrs Caldicot wondered why even doctors couldn't bring themselves to talk directly about death, and then she suddenly remembered where she had seen him before. He had been on the local television station taking part in a discussion programme about the psychological problems created by bereavement and the failure of modern society to take these problems seriously.

`She's been behaving very strangely,' Veronica whispered to the doctor, as though she did not expect Mrs Caldicot to be able to hear her. `We've found her a really lovely home to move into – The Twilight Years Rest Home it's called – but she says she doesn't want to go!'

The doctor, listening to Veronica, nodded and grunted in Mrs Caldicot's direction, looking at her critically and suspiciously.

`She can't stay here!' insisted Veronica, still speaking in a perfectly audible whisper. `Vandals!' she explained. `They've already been round here once.' She related in exaggerated and much rehearsed detail the saga of the chrysanthemums. By now the vandals responsible for this act of premeditated violence had arrived on motorcycles, had brandished machetes and had threatened Mrs Caldicot with a fate worse than death.

'Why don't you want to go to this nice home your relatives have found for you?' asked the doctor, as though Mrs Caldicot's had chosen to turn down a gift of a million pounds, a villa in the South of France and a lifetime's supply of champagne.

Mrs Caldicot stared at him and wondered how anyone so unintelligent and unperceptive could have attained a position of such responsibility. 'How would you like it,' she thought, 'if your relatives turned up one day and insisted that you had to sell up your home and move into a Salvation Army hostel?' She thought this but said nothing.

'I know Mr Fuller-Hawksmoor of The Twilight Years,' said the doctor. 'He's a splendid fellow. Heart in absolutely the right place.'

'The right place for his heart would be someone else's body,' thought Mrs Caldicot.

'They'll provide all your meals and look after your laundry,' continued the doctor. 'They'll take complete care of you, and you won't have to worry about being a burden on your relatives.'

'Why,' wondered Mrs Caldicot, 'do people assume that I am suddenly incapable of looking after myself? Up until a few days ago I looked after myself and my husband. I did all my own shopping, cooking, cleaning and laundry. Now, suddenly I need to be put into a home.' She did not say any of this.

'That's another thing,' murmured Veronica, as though by speaking quietly she could ensure that she would not be overhead by her mother-in-law, 'most of the time when you talk to her she doesn't say anything. You can tell she's heard you and you know she's thinking, but she doesn't say anything.' Veronica paused and pursed her lips as though she had vinegar in her mouth. 'It's very disconcerting.'

Mrs Caldicot, who had for years chosen to keep her thoughts to herself and who had put up with the inane and pointless blathering of those around her, listened to this criticism resignedly. She kept silent not because she couldn't think of anything to say, but because she couldn't see the point in saying what she'd thought. She had long ago realised that her husband and her daughter-in-law had the combined intelligence of a potato peeler, and rather than waste her time on pointless conversations she preferred to remain silent. Over the years she had got quite good at it. She could hear what people were saying to her, of course. And she formulated replies in her own mind.

Replies which were unconstrained by social niceties and were, therefore, simple and honest. But whatever the temptation or provocation she had rarely opened her mouth apart from to communicate specific information. She was honest to herself but not necessarily to others.

The doctor, unworried by Mrs Caldicot's silence, which he mistook for a mixture of deference and depression, nodded sagely. `I can give you a little something to help you over these difficult days,' he said, speaking to Mrs Caldicot with what she supposed was his sympathetic look. He took out his pen, a cheap, white plastic instrument with the name of a pharmaceutical product emblazoned on the side in bold blue lettering, and started to write a prescription in one slick, well-practised movement. As he did so Mrs Caldicot found herself wondering if doctors had competitions to see which of them could draw a pen and write a prescription the fastest.

The doctor finished the prescription writing, put his pen away and handed the completed form to Veronica. `Just one tablet three times a day,' he murmured, speaking to Veronica as though unwilling to entrust Mrs Caldicot with these complicated and important instructions. `They'll help her behave a little more rationally.'

`I'll see that she takes them, doctor,' promised Veronica, accepting the prescription as though it were an award. Mrs Caldicot rather thought that her daughter-in-law might have curtsied had the doctor not thwarted this by picking up his unopened bag and heading speedily towards the door.

Mrs Caldicot turned back to look through the living room window and was glad she did so for the rain was now coming down more heavily than ever. She saw Derek, who was clearly soaked, slip and drop the bundle of canes he was holding, falling face down into the mud. It was, thought Mrs Caldicot, the most graceful thing he had ever done.

For the first time in many months Mrs Caldicot laughed out loud. Although the laugh did not last long, the incident cheered her up for a moment, and she could not help thinking how therapeutic a moment of laughter can be. She realised with some sadness that it was the first time that her son had ever made her laugh, but underneath it she felt a sadness and despair. What she really wanted, she decided, was time to think and time to come to terms with what had happened, time to re-plan her life and time to think about the future.

But people seemed keen only to offer her advice; time was the one thing no one wanted to allow her.

CHAPTER NINE

Mrs Caldicot sat in the back of Derek's motor car and stared at the back of Veronica's neck trying to decide whether or not to be sick.

The tablets which the doctor had prescribed for her, and which Veronica and Derek had made sure that she had taken, had a number of unpleasant physical side effects among which indigestion, headaches, dizziness and nausea were most prominent. They had also made her feel extremely drowsy, and everything that had happened to her since she had started to take them had taken place in a thick mist which had slowed both her perceptions and her actions. Despite all these side effects the tablets had not affected Mrs Caldicot's colicky pains which remained as strong, as persistent and as unpredictable as ever.

The car stopped with a shudder and Mrs Caldicot, looking out through the rear window with dull eyes, recognised the front steps but could not remember precisely why.

`Come on, mother!' said Derek cheerily. He held open the car door and offered Mrs Caldicot his hand. Cautiously, hesitantly, Mrs Caldicot moved her legs and swung them out of the car. They felt as though they were separated in some way from the rest of her body and she watched them move with some surprise and a little relief. She felt overcome by physical tiredness, though she dimly realised, with some relief, that the intense almost suffocating feeling of dizziness which she had experienced a few moments earlier had subsided a little.

It seemed to take her an age to walk from the car to the bottom of the stone steps and another lifetime to climb them. By the time she, Derek, Veronica and Jason stood together outside the front door of The Twilight Years Rest Home Mrs Caldicot had become so depressed by her lack of strength and energy that she felt tears rolling down her cheeks. Through the sadness and the weakness and the mist in her mind she vowed to herself that she would take no more of the pills she had been given. Derek, seeing the tears streaming down his mother's cheeks turned away in embarrassment assuming, quite wrongly, that the tears were inspired either by apprehension or regret.

The rest of that day passed by Mrs Caldicot in a blur. It was almost as though her body had been taken over by someone else, and she was standing to one side watching as an only partly interested spectator.

***

Much, much later, she awoke to find herself lying flat on her back in bed. She was aware that she could hear someone else in the room but she kept her eyes closed and lay still and silent, trying to get her bearings.

`Come on!' she heard someone say. `Time you were up! Breakfast in fifteen minutes.'

She opened her eyes. A large, shapeless woman in a white overall was standing by the side of her bed.

`Take this!' said the woman in the white overall, thrusting a capsule in Mrs Caldicot's direction.

Mrs Caldicot stared at it for a moment without moving.

`Open your mouth!' instructed the woman in the white overall.

Mrs Caldicot did as she was told and the woman in the white overall popped the capsule into her mouth before moving on to the next bed.

Carefully making sure that she did not swallow the capsule Mrs Caldicot watched the woman give something to each of the two other residents in the room, then open the door and leave. Only then did she spit the capsule into her hand, ease her stiff body out of bed, walk slowly across the room to the sink and wash the capsule away down the plughole.

***

It took most of the day for the effects of the previous day's drugs to wear off, and by dinner that evening Mrs Caldicot was beginning to feel almost human again. She still had a mild headache, she still felt slightly nauseated and she still felt a little sleepy, but the worst of the thick mist had dispersed.

It had not, however, taken Mrs Caldicot that long to realise that The Twilight Years Rest Home was a considerably different place when seen through the eyes of a resident compared to when it was viewed through the eyes of a visitor.

Most noticeable was the enormous difference in the behaviour of the proprietor, Mr Fuller-Hawksmoor.

When Mrs Caldicot had been a *prospective* resident, accompanied by her family, Mr Fuller-Hawksmoor had attempted to give the impression of being a kindly, humane, fairly patient sort of fellow. But when Mrs Caldicot had become a resident Mr Fuller-Hawksmoor had become a very different character; all pretence at a generous, sensitive nature abandoned.

She spent the next morning sitting in the lounge. She did not know what she ate for lunch. Apart from half a plateful of pale and watery cabbage she found it impossible to identify the constituents of her meal.

In the afternoon she returned to the lounge where she sat in an uncomfortable communal silence; a silence broken only by the loud breathing of several residents who had temporarily escaped from drug-induced consciousness to drug-induced unconsciousness without apparently attracting any concern from Mr Fuller-Hawksmoor and his highly-trained staff.

And in the evening she returned to the dining room only to be repelled by an unrequested reprise of lunchtime's dominant and malodorous vegetable.

Feeling her stomach churning and her appetite gone Mrs Caldicot turned to leave the dining room and found herself being called back by Mr Fuller-Hawksmoor.

`Where are you going, mother?' called Mr Fuller-Hawksmoor, who used this term of reference when addressing all his female residents (strangely and unevenly he referred to the men as `dad').

For a moment Mrs Caldicot, who was not sure that Mr Fuller-Hawksmoor was addressing her, failed to respond. She quite rightly assumed that even if he was talking to her he was using this familial form of address solely because he could not be bothered to remember her name; and her dignity, although it had been threatened, savaged and beaten had not yet been dissembled.

Mr Fuller-Hawksmoor repeated himself, speaking if anything a little louder than before. He spoke to his residents in the same way that Veronica Caldicot would speak to a foreigner: assuming that all misunderstandings and communication failures could be remedied simply by turning up the volume.

Mrs Caldicot turned and stared at him coldly. For years and years she had been put upon, talked down to, bullied and pushed around. She had spent her life doing what other people wanted her to do, and saying what she felt other people expected her to say. She suddenly felt angry and indignant and realised that she had nothing to lose.

Later, she wondered if the remnants of the drugs had influenced her at that moment; covering up her overdeveloped sense of social obedience and releasing the tiger within her which had lain dormant for so many years.

`Mr Fuller-Hawksmoor,' she thought and said, `I don't want to eat your cabbage. Moreover, to the best of my knowledge I am not your mother and I would, therefore, be grateful if you would stop calling me `mother'.' She paused briefly to allow her words to sink in. `My friends call me Thelma but you can call me Mrs Caldicot.'

She thought and said!

She said!

For a brief moment Mrs Caldicot was not even sure that she had said what she had thought. She was so accustomed to thinking things but not saying things that for an instant she did not realise that she had actually shared her private thoughts with the obnoxious Mr Fuller-Hawksmoor. For years she had been inhibited, frustrated and thwarted by a husband who had filled her life like stale, stuffy air fills a room the morning after a party. Even after he had gone, her husband's influence had clung to her like a pall of cigarette smoke. She waited for her colicky abdominal pains to begin.

Then, the moment the look on Mr Fuller-Hawksmoor's face confirmed that she had indeed said what she had thought, Mrs Caldicot felt herself blushing deeply. Never before had she defended herself with such certainty. Never before had her spirit and her body united in such a single minded display of solidarity. Her heart beat faster and faster until she feared that it would burst from her chest. She felt the tiny hairs on the back of her neck stand up. Her palms felt damp and clammy. She had always kept her thoughts to herself; every emotion she felt, every instinct for self defence, had always been overshadowed by an overpowering sense of obedience, an unwillingness to disappoint or upset those around her and a matching desire to please. She made a vow not to waste any more of her life on mealy mouthed compromises and hypocrisy, on social courtesy and dishonest politesse.

Mr Fuller-Hawksmoor stared at her for several moments, clearly unaccustomed to being spoken to in such a manner and just as clearly quite uncertain about what to say in response. He opened his mouth for an instant, as though about to quell this rebellious mischief maker with a neatly crafted barb. But although his mouth was open no sound came from it. Mr Fuller-Hawksmoor was, quite literally, lost for words.

And then, to both Mr Fuller-Hawksmoor's and Mrs Caldicot's surprise, the other residents, at least all of the ones who had overheard this very one-sided exchange, burst into a spontaneous round of applause. It was not, it is true, the sort of applause that you are likely to hear at Lord's Cricket Ground on a balmy summer's afternoon when a batsman has scored a spectacular century. But then the audience was severely disadvantaged, both in terms of numbers and physical ability. It takes two healthy arms and two healthy hands, preferably with the requisite number of fingers, to produce a decent burst of applause, and the residents of The Twilight Years Rest Home were almost unanimously deprived of these essential physical constituents. Still, they did their best with their arthritic fingers, wrists and elbows, and those enthusiasts who were unable to applaud in the usual way banged their walking sticks on the floor or scratched their walking frames backwards and forwards. They had been mistreated and deprived of their dignity by Mr Fuller-Hawksmoor, and Mrs Caldicot's moment of rebellion had brought them together in a glorious spirit of revolution.

Normally, at precious moments like this, there is a temptation to spoil the perfection; to try to add another layer to the card house. But Mrs Caldicot, as though naturally aware that another word from her would have turned the put-down into a mere conversational gambit, resisted the temptation to say anything else. Instead she turned and, head held high, headed for the stairs and the relative seclusion, privacy and safety of her one third of The Windsor Suite.

She sat in her room and thought of all the times she had said (or thought) `I wish I had done that' or `If only...' and then she thought of all the times she had said `I wish I hadn't done that' or `I wish I hadn't said that' and she realised that the regrets from the former far outweighed the regrets from the latter.

She also realised, with some surprise, that she had suffered no pains in her abdomen. Her colic seemed to have been banished by her honesty. To her surprise and delight it did not return.

CHAPTER TEN

Mrs Caldicot, who had become something of a heroine to the residents of The Twilight Years Rest Home (but a dangerous anarchist to the proprietor), quickly found that she had now burnt her boats, destroyed her bridges and cut off her retreat. She had made her bed and now she had to lie on it (or, more commonly, at least during the daytime hours, sit on it).

`I suppose you think you're clever,' hissed Mr Fuller-Hawksmoor, bursting into The Windsor Suite a few minutes after Mrs Caldicot's memorable defiance and looking for all the world like a stage villain in a children's pantomime as he glowered at her.

`It's all relative,' thought and said Mrs Caldicot, now freed of her reluctance to speak, `Compared to Einstein I'm not clever.' She shrugged. `But...'

`Don't you try to get the better of me!' threatened Mr Fuller-Hawksmoor, waving a podgy finger. `If you do you'll soon find out who's the boss around here.'

Mrs Caldicot smiled at him, raised an eyebrow and turned away. The message was clear. Mr Fuller-Hawksmoor left.

**

Mrs Caldicot pounced on Derek and Veronica when they arrived to see her that first evening. (Jason had come with them but, thought Mrs Caldicot, only in the sort of way that a bad odour will follow its human source).

`Where's Kitty?' Mrs Caldicot demanded. `And what have you done to my house? What about all my furniture? My clothes? And everything else?'

`Now don't you worry about a thing, mother,' said Derek, closing his eyes in that way that people do when they are embarrassed and don't want to look at the person they are talking to. He held up what he thought was a calming hand. `Everything,' he said with a glorious overstatement, `is under control. I've put the house on the market and we've organised an auction for your furniture.'

Mrs Caldicot knew that if Derek was in charge, `control' was not a word to be used without a considerable number of qualifications, and so she was not to be easily distracted from her investigation. `Who gave you permission to sell my house?' she wanted to ask. `Who said you could sell my furniture?'

`Where is Kitty?' she demanded firmly, putting first things first.

`Kitty is fine,' said Veronica, who was wearing a black and yellow houndstooth check suit, a pink man-made fibre scarf and a pillar box red hat. `She's in a lovely home too.'

`Where?' asked Mrs Caldicot.

`The Sleepy Pussy Cattery,' replied Veronica. `It's very expensive so it must be good.' She twisted her mouth as she said this, giving the clear impression that she considered the price that was being paid for Kitty's welfare to be absurdly wasteful and Mrs Caldicot knew in her heart that if Veronica was left in charge she would soon find an excuse to take Kitty on a one way trip to see the veterinary surgeon.

`And that,' said Mrs Caldicot rejoicing in her new found freedom of expression and wondering why she had spent so many years thinking things and not saying them, `just about sums you up, Veronica!' Mrs Caldicot had never liked Veronica much and found her ready willingness to equate price with quality a suitable indictment of her intelligence.

`I want Kitty here, with me,' she said, firmly.

Veronica, deflated by this unexpected firmness, stepped backwards a pace and opened her mouth as though she had entered a fly catching contest. Mrs Caldicot thought that her daughter- in-law's response reminded her very much of that of Mr Fuller-Hawksmoor.

`Oh good heavens, mother!' said Derek. `You can't have a cat living with you in a hospital.'

`This isn't a hospital!' Mrs Caldicot pointed out. `When you first brought me here you told me quite specifically that it wasn't a hospital. What's more it doesn't smell like a hospital and it isn't run like a hospital.'

`I don't think it would be fair to the other patients to bring a cat here,' said Veronica, who had made a temporary recovery and was now speaking in what she clearly thought was a whisper, though as a whisper it would have been more at home on a stage than in a boudoir.

`Oh do shut up, Veronica!' said Mrs Caldicot, surprising herself yet again.

`I'll see what Mr Fuller-Hawksmoor has to say,' sighed Derek, heading for the door.

`If I stay here I'm having Kitty here to live with me,' said Mrs Caldicot. `She can have a litter tray in our room and she won't be any bother to anyone else.'

**

After that bold and successful stance Mrs Caldicot decided to spend her time in her room getting to know her companions a little better.

The two other beds in The Windsor Suite were occupied by Miss Nightingale and Mrs Peterborough. Miss Nightingale was the elderly, bed bound lady needing a bedpan whom Mrs Caldicot had seen on her first visit. Mrs Peterborough was an unremittingly talkative woman; a physically much more robust individual than Miss Nightingale who, as the result of some mysterious, cortical disorder had acquired a personality like a piece of blotting paper.

Mrs Caldicot had originally assumed that Miss Nightingale spent her days as well as her nights in bed because of some physical disability, but this was not the case. Miss Nightingale, was, like so many elderly people (and Miss Nightingale, having enjoyed her eightieth birthday some months previously was not shy about describing herself as elderly) a mild, modest and innocent victim of a disease which used to be known as senile dementia but which is now more usually classified (with the appropriate enhancement of status) as Alzheimer's Disease.

The two main consequences of Miss Nightingale's disability were confusion and memory loss, though the problems created by these symptoms were exacerbated enormously by their unpredictability. One moment Miss Nightingale would talk cogently and wittily about the decline in the status and morals of the British Royal Family while the next she would slip back into some childhood drama and lose all contact with reality; it was as though she were forever playing some large as life game of snakes and ladders, clambering up ladders to momentary sanity and then sliding down snakes into temporary insanity while fate threw the dice for her.

These unpredictable mental forays worried the establishment at The Twilight Years Rest Home and, arguing that they regarded Miss

Nightingale's mental condition as potentially disturbing for the other residents Mr Fuller-Hawksmoor and his staff kept her constantly sedated and effectively imprisoned with a confusion of powerful tranquillisers and sedatives.

Suspecting that Miss Nightingale's physical weakness was probably a consequence rather than a cause of the long hours she spent in bed, and knowing from her own experience that the tranquillising tablets she had been given had weakened her spirit, muddled her mind and muddied her capacity for clear thinking, Mrs Caldicot decided to try to resuscitate her elderly roommate by helping her to stop taking her medication.

Mrs Caldicot had stopped taking her pills the day she had entered the rest home, and although the nursing auxiliaries still gave her pills, which she took from them with a suitably blank smile, she regularly washed them down the plug hole of the bedroom wash basin.

She now set about the task of helping Miss Nightingale to escape from her pharmacological imprisonment. To do this was easier than she had expected. She ingratiated herself with the auxiliaries who were eager to hand over one of their tedious chores and to escape to their rest-room a few minutes earlier than planned to enjoy an illicit cigarette and a gossip about the comings and doings of the latest television celebrities. The auxiliaries were to start with suspicious of Mrs Caldicot after her outburst outside the dining room, but they were at the same time secretly pleased that their tyrannical employer had been put in his place and they did not mind making friends with his conqueror. Within three days of arriving at the rest home Mrs Caldicot had taken on the responsibility for giving Miss Nightingale all her pills. This meant that several times a day a colourful mixture of tablets and capsules were washed down the wash basin plug hole.

Mrs Caldicot found that the hardest part of her enterprise was persuading Miss Nightingale to pretend that she was still under the influence of her pills.

As the mist of drug-induced depression lifted from her mind Miss Nightingale grew gradually more and more lively and increasingly alert. Instead of lying still in her bed, as inert and as full of sparks as a rubber hot water bottle, Miss Nightingale began to waken, as though from a deep slumber.

Mrs Caldicot quickly found that one way to suppress Miss

Nightingale's newly found propensity to chatter incessantly and unpredictably about anything and everything was to tire her out; to exhaust her physically so that she fell into a genuine sleep at night. To do this she conducted impromptu exercise classes in The Windsor Suite. At first, Miss Nightingale could not stand without help, but within two days she could walk by herself and within a week she could perform a determined and spirited, if slightly uncoordinated, jig to the music that Mrs Caldicot played on her small tape player.

Miss Nightingale loved these simple exercises and although she may not have the sort of reliable intellect, regard for temporal or spatial rules or sense of logical continuity that one would normally expect in, say, an accountant or a judge, Mrs Caldicot could see that Miss Nightingale was coming back to life. The third resident of The Windsor Suite, Mrs Peterborough, whose daily medication had been similarly hi-jacked by Mrs Caldicot, also enjoyed these impromptu exercise classes.

Mrs Peterborough's mental condition was, in some ways, potentially far more disturbing for the residents than Miss Nightingale's, but neither Mr Fuller-Hawksmoor nor the medical advisers who regularly visited the home to hand out prescriptions for newer and ever more powerful pharmacological truncheons, had yet managed to find anything strong enough to quell her mental status without at the same time rendering her completely unconscious (this was considered an unacceptable alternative, not because of any respect for Mrs Peterborough's rights but because unconscious patients need very concentrated nursing care, and very concentrated nursing care costs a lot of money).

Each one of us has a personality which we and our friends grow to recognise. Most of us wake up each morning knowing who we are and roughly how we will respond to the people and the problems we meet.

This was not, however, the case with Mrs Peterborough. She woke each morning with no fixed personality but with a fresh, blank canvas upon which would be painted a series of personality caricatures derived entirely from her worldly experiences and mirroring, often with unerring accuracy, the personalities and moods of people whom she encountered. The stronger the personality or the more determined the mood she encountered the more Mrs

Peterborough was likely to adopt it. If someone was cruel to her she would be cruel to them. If someone was kind to her she would be kind to them. Everyone who came into contact with her reaped exactly as they sowed; although some confusion was created by the fact that if she watched television Mrs Peterborough would quickly adopt the personality of the most powerful character on the screen. Life with Mrs Peterborough was made even more complicated by the fact that she had a habit of repeating everything that was said to her. She was a vocal mirror; a human tape recorder set constantly on record and replay.

**

Next door to The Windsor Suite was The Duchy of Cornwall Suite, shared by Mr Hewitt and Mr Livingstone.

Mr Hewitt was 92-years-old and proud of it. He had worked as a gardener all his adult life and had only stopped working when his granddaughter and her husband, who were both solicitors, had decided that he was too old to work. Ignoring his protests they had written to his employer warning him of the dangers of employing such an elderly pensioner, had ended his tenancy of a cottage on a nearby estate and had placed him in The Twilight Years Rest Home. They had even sold his beloved gardening tools (though Mr Hewitt had rescued a small trowel, a hand fork and a wooden dibber and he kept these three instruments, oiled and wrapped in a piece of dark green canvas, in the bottom of his bedside locker).

Mr Hewitt desperately missed managing a garden and had, he told Mrs Caldicot, on several occasions begged Mr Fuller-Hawksmoor to be allowed to dig up and cultivate a small portion of the lawn around the home. Mr Fuller-Hawksmoor had summarily rejected these entreaties claiming that relatives wouldn't pay him good money if they saw old people getting sweaty and dirty in the garden.

`But I like getting sweaty and dirty,' protested Mr Hewitt to Mrs Caldicot. `It's what I do best!'

Compared to Mr Hewitt, Mr Livingstone was a mere youngster, having recently celebrated his 75th birthday. Mr Hewitt had been at work for five years when his junior room-mate had been born.

At heart Mr Livingstone was a musician.

He had not, however, earned his living as a musician because his wife, a nervous sort long since passed away, had never thought a career in a jazz band a stable enough way to bring up three children and pay the household bills. And so for fifty years Mr Livingstone, a loyal and selfless husband and father, had spent the best waking hours of his life working as a wages clerk for a factory making cardboard boxes.

But in his heart he always thought of himself as a musician and still described himself as such when anyone bothered to ask. He could play the piano, the flute, the trombone and the drums, but Mr Fuller-Hawksmoor would not allow him to practise any of these instruments because, he said, the noise might prove disturbing. Even when the other residents made it clear that they didn't mind the noise Mr Fuller-Hawksmoor remained unmoved, unmoving and unmoveable. Deprived of the chance to make music Mr Livingstone was slowly drifting into a slough of despair.

And so, it was in this way that Mrs Caldicot passed her first few weeks in The Twilight Years Rest Home: getting to know and to love her new friends. She felt fitter, stronger and happier than she had for years.

CHAPTER ELEVEN

Mr Fuller-Hawksmoor didn't like Mrs Caldicot and would not willingly have done her any favours. When he had reluctantly agreed to allow Mrs Caldicot to keep her cat in The Windsor Suite he had done so only because he was primarily a businessman and his affection for money outweighed his pride and yearning for vengeance. He didn't want to risk calling Mrs Caldicot's bluff and seeing her leave the nursing home.

But he knew that he only had to be patient and his time would come. And he did not have to wait very long.

A month after Mrs Caldicot (and Kitty) had moved into The Twilight Years Rest Home Mr Fuller-Hawksmoor was approached by another family looking for somewhere for an elderly female relative to stay. Mr Fuller-Hawksmoor knew that this was the moment he had been waiting for; having another potential resident to fill Mrs Caldicot's bed gave him a chance to be tough without having to risk any financial loss.

`I allowed you to keep your cat in the suite for a trial period,' he said to Mrs Caldicot. `But I'm afraid that the trial period is over and the cat will have to go.'

Mrs Caldicot was shocked but not entirely surprised. `You didn't say anything about a trial period,' she protested, accurately.

`I want the cat out by tomorrow night,' said Mr Fuller-Hawksmoor, ignoring Mrs Caldicot's protest.

`Have there been any complaints?' asked Mrs Caldicot, knowing full well that there hadn't been.

`I'm afraid I can't answer that,' said Mr Fuller-Hawksmoor coldly and pompously. `It would be a breach of confidence.'

`And just where is Kitty supposed to go?' asked Mrs Caldicot.

Mr Fuller-Hawksmoor shrugged. `I don't care where she goes,' he said callously. `You can send her to a cattery or have her put down by the vet for all I care. But I don't want her here.' And with that he turned and stalked off. `Don't forget,' he added, turning his head as he walked away, `I want the cat out by tomorrow night.'

Mrs Caldicot, who had shivered with anger and horror at the

phrase `put down by the vet' stared after him. `If she goes then I go,' she said loudly and firmly. She had long ago weighed up Mr Fuller-Hawksmoor accurately. She believed that he was far too greedy to risk losing her weekly cheque, and she felt certain that she had the upper hand. Sadly, for her, she had no way of knowing that there was another potential resident waiting to take her place and that, therefore, her threat was an empty one.

Mr Fuller-Hawksmoor retraced his steps so that he was standing no more than a yard or two away from Mrs Caldicot. `Fine,' he said, clearly savouring the moment. `Please vacate your room by noon tomorrow.'

To say that this both shocked and startled Mrs Caldicot would be an understatement of heroic proportions. Although she did not like The Twilight Years Rest Home the truth was that Mrs Caldicot had nowhere else to go. Her son, Derek, had put her house on the market even before she had left it; the furniture had been sold at auction and her few remaining private possessions were now stored in a trunk in Derek and Veronica's garage.

But Mrs Caldicot was not going to let Mr Fuller-Hawksmoor know that his calling of her bluff had discomforted her. `It will be my pleasure,' she said with apparent sincerity, fervently hoping that Mr Fuller-Hawksmoor could not hear her pounding heart and praying that whatever happened she would not collapse in front of him. `If the shock of this has to kill me,' she prayed silently, `please let me survive until I've got out of this place. I don't want to give Fuller-Hawksmoor the satisfaction of knowing that he's upset me.'

***

`But you can't go!' sobbed Miss Nightingale, when Mrs Caldicot told her that she and Kitty were leaving. With Mrs Caldicot's help Miss Nightingale had made enormous progress, and although she had still not ventured outside The Windsor Suite she had become physically independent. She was still forgetful and occasionally confused and she wandered freely through time but instead of being a bed-bound lunatic she was now merely a rather eccentric and frail old lady.

`You can't go! You mustn't go!' said Mrs Peterborough, mimicking Miss Nightingale and bursting into tears.

`I've got to leave,' insisted Mrs Caldicot quietly. She was holding

Kitty who was purring contentedly in her arms.

She still had no idea where she would go but for the moment that was the least of her problems. She walked across to the television set, switched it on and flicked through the channels until she found the calming and reassuring face of a woman presenting an anodyne programme made by brain dead producers for brain dead housewives. The television repair man had managed to get a picture out of the elderly set but he hadn't managed to find all the colours; the result was that everything and everyone on the screen appeared to be suffering from a rather severe case of sunburn. Mrs Caldicot adjusted the volume so that it could only just be heard and put a kindly arm around Mrs Peterborough's shoulders. `Sit and watch this!' she murmured, knowing from experience that Mrs Peterborough would soon match the mood of the soothing presenter. Once, before she had realised just how closely Mrs Peterborough's moods and emotions mirrored those which she saw, she had left her watching a Tom and Jerry cartoon. She had come back to find Mrs Peterborough sitting grinning in the middle of the floor surrounded by torn bedclothes, broken bric a brac and many other signs of mayhem. She had, since then, been careful to make sure that she never left Mrs Peterborough watching any cartoon programmes or any programmes which contained any elements of violence or unpredictability. She put Kitty down on the bed and started gathering together her few belongings, packing them into a battered blue cardboard suitcase which she had pulled out from underneath her bed.

`But you're my friend!' said Miss Nightingale, sitting sadly on the edge of her own bed and moodily banging her heels onto the carpet. `What on earth will I do without you?'

`Add two spoonfuls of olive oil and a splash of vinegar,' nodded Mrs Peterborough faithfully, carefully watching the television presenter and even managing to sound uncannily like her.

`What about my exercises?' asked Miss Nightingale, plaintively. `I like doing my exercises!'

`I'll show you how to work the tape player and you can do them by yourself,' promised Mrs Caldicot.

`It won't be the same,' insisted Miss Nightingale, miserably.

`Stir the mixture well and put it into a warm oven for twenty minutes,' said Mrs Peterborough, nodding happily and smiling vacuously.

'I wanted you to come home with me in the summer holidays to meet my parents,' said Miss Nightingale sadly.

'Mmmmm!' said Mrs Peterborough. 'And the finished dish smells and tastes absolutely wonderful – especially with a slice of garlic bread!' She licked her lips and smiled back at the screen.

'That's kind of you,' said Mrs Caldicot, who knew that Miss Nightingale's parents had both been dead for thirty years. 'Another time, maybe?'

'And now we're going to see what Amanda has got for us this week,' said Mrs Peterborough.

'You've been such a good friend to me,' said Miss Nightingale, who had started to cry again. 'No one else would ever share their tuck box but you always would.'

'We'll see each other again,' said Mrs Caldicot reassuringly. She sat down beside Miss Nightingale and put her arm around her. 'In the holidays,' she added hopefully.

'I wish you didn't have to go,' sobbed Miss Nightingale. She suddenly looked confused. 'What holidays?' she asked. 'Are we going on holiday? To Tenby?'

'Hello! I'm Amanda!' said Mrs Peterborough, sounding like a bright and high-spirited 18-year-old. 'I've been to Staffordshire to meet a man who trains women how to defend themselves against attackers! He's going to show me how to throw a fourteen stone man over my shoulder!'

Miss Nightingale stopped crying. 'I've had a wonderful idea!' she said, brightly. 'I'll come with you!'

Mrs Caldicot stood up, walked quickly over to the television set and switched channels.

Kitty leapt into Mrs Caldicot's open suitcase and started treadling on a couple of jumpers.

'....e.x.t.e.r.m.i.n.a.t.e...e.x.t.e.r.m.i.n.a.t.e...' said Mrs Peterborough, mimicking a Dalek on a re-run of an old Dr Who programme. 'We will e.x.t.e.r.m.i.n.a.t.e. you...'

'Click!' as Mrs Caldicot switched channels.

'Have you seen my suitcase?' asked Miss Nightingale, down on her hands and knees and looking underneath her bed.

'...one move out of you and you're dead!' said Mrs Peterborough, gruffly, narrowing her eyes to guard against the desert sun and holding her right hand an inch above her gun holster.

`Click!' as Mrs Caldicot switched channels.

`I don't want to take any of my rubbish with me anyway,' said Miss Nightingale, slumping down on her bed, already weary of the search. `Where are we going?' she asked brightly.

`...the gardens on Tresco are among the most wonderful and peaceful in the world, especially at this time of the year,' said Mrs Peterborough soothingly. `Look at this wonderful example of the Sparmannia africana! I've got one at home growing in a small pot. Here they've got one that is three metres high!'

Mrs Caldicot sighed and moved away from the television set. `You can't come with me, Miss Nightingale!' she said quietly. `I'm sorry!'

Kitty miaowed in complaint as Mrs Caldicot lifted her out of the suitcase so that she could carry on with her packing.

`It's very sad,' said Miss Nightingale.

`Now we're going over to Samantha back in the studio,' said Mrs Peterborough. `She's going to show us this season's range of super new lipsticks.'

CHAPTER TWELVE

Mrs Caldicot fully intended to leave The Twilight Years Rest Home quietly and with dignity.

At ten o'clock the following morning she walked down the stairs of the home with her blue cardboard suitcase in her left hand and Kitty's basket in her right.

But her departure didn't go quite the way she expected.

Miss Nightingale was the first to follow her. She had wrapped herself in a pink woollen dressing gown which had tiny yellow flowers on the breast pocket, slipped into her only pair of outdoor shoes and, carrying her handbag, tip-toed down the stairs behind Mrs Caldicot. In the handbag she had carefully and thoughtfully packed her alarm clock, a roll of soft toilet paper, three humbugs and a slice of bread which she had found in her bedside locker.

Behind Miss Nightingale came Mrs Peterborough.

She too was wearing her dressing gown and a pair of outdoor shoes but she couldn't find her handbag and so, instead, she was carrying an empty metal kidney dish.

As this small and rather bizarre procession reached the bottom of the stairs Mr Fuller-Hawksmoor appeared as if from nowhere (though in truth he had been skulking in the dining room waiting to make sure that Mrs Caldicot really did leave) and stood in front of Mrs Caldicot with his arms folded across his chest.

`So!' he said, `You're leaving!'

`We are!' said Mrs Caldicot firmly.

`We?' said Mr Fuller-Hawksmoor, suddenly looking worried. `What do you mean by `we'?'

`Kitty and I,' said Mrs Caldicot.

`And me!' piped up Miss Nightingale, `I'm going with her!'

`And me!' mimicked Mrs Peterborough. `I'm going with her!'

Mrs Caldicot, who had not been aware that her two room-mates had been following her and who was startled by this new development, was speechless. Mr Fuller-Hawksmoor, seeing his income about to fall dramatically, was not. `No you're jolly well not!' he shouted angrily, and this was his downfall, for his loudly voiced anger provoked an immediate, noisy and attention-attracting response from Mrs Caldicot's acolytes.

`You can't stop us!' said Miss Nightingale, defiantly.

`You can't stop us! You jolly well can't!' shouted Mrs Peterborough, getting slightly confused but managing, nevertheless, to stay within the spirit of the conversation. Her voice carried considerably further than that of Miss Nightingale.

`Mrs Caldicot's leaving!' cried someone standing unseen above them on the staircase.

`They're leaving!' shouted someone else.

`We're all leaving!' said Miss Nightingale.

`We're all leaving!' shouted Mrs Peterborough.

`We're all leaving!' shouted a third unseen patient.

`Wait for me!' shouted a fourth. `I want to come too.'

`If Mrs Caldicot is going I'm going too,' said Mr Hewitt, rushing back to The Duchy of Cornwall Suite to collect his precious parcel of gardening tools.

`Wait for me!' cried Mr Livingstone.

Within moments The Twilight Years Rest Home was full of elderly patients rushing around in their pyjamas and their nightdresses looking for dressing gowns and shoes and handbags and suitcases and shouting to Mrs Caldicot to wait for them and shouting at Mr Fuller-Hawksmoor who was screaming at them to tell them they couldn't leave. Mrs Caldicot had become more than just a friend to all of these old people; she had become a symbol of hope. They liked her, they trusted her and they had faith in her. She was the only person in the home who had ever had the courage to stand up to Mr Fuller-Hawksmoor's bullying and they admired and respected her for that.

`Oh dear,' said Mrs Caldicot, to no one in particular. `Oh dear me.' She started to move towards the front door but the anguished cries of `Wait for me!' and `Don't go yet!' which filled the hallway and echoed up and down the staircase halted her.

`But you can't come with me,' said Mrs Caldicot to Miss Nightingale. `I don't know where I'm going!'

`I don't want to stay here by myself,' insisted Miss Nightingale.

`I don't want to stay here by myself,' echoed Mrs Peterborough.

`You can't come out into the cold dressed like that,' said Mrs Caldicot sensibly. `You'll catch your death of cold!'

`I've got a coat!' said Miss Nightingale. And with that she turned and ran back upstairs. `She said I can go with her if I put my coat on!' she shouted.

`I can go with her if I put my coat on!' shouted Mrs Peterborough gleefully following Miss Nightingale back upstairs.

`We can go with her if we put our coats on!' cried someone else, and a dozen septuagenarians and octogenarians rushed back up to their rooms to fetch their coats.

`You'll be responsible if anything happens to any of these people!' said Mr Fuller-Hawksmoor, a tiny fleck of spittle appearing at the corner of his mouth as he worked himself up into a considerable state of excitement.

`No I won't!' replied Mrs Caldicot. `They're all old enough to know what they're doing. And I didn't ask any of them to come with me.'

`I'm going to ring your son!' threatened Mr Fuller-Hawksmoor. `Let's see what he has to say about this!'

Mrs Caldicot, who regarded her son as about as threatening as the Sugar Plum Fairy, stared at Mr Fuller-Hawksmoor. The nursing home proprietor, quelled by the fierceness of Mrs Caldicot's glare, withered where he stood.

A few minutes later Mrs Caldicot, who had, if the truth be known, felt just a teeny bit alone and just a weeny, little bit afraid and uncertain when she had started her journey down the staircase towards the front door and freedom, left The Twilight Years Rest Home at the head of an untidy and straggling procession of chattering and excited escapees. The few residents who were physically incapable of leaving the building shouted encouragement from their beds and wheelchairs, and although they were sad at not being able to join the exodus they clearly shared the sense of excitement at what was going on.

Mrs Caldicot felt a strange mixture of embarrassment (not at heading such a motley crew but at being the instigator of such a momentous exodus) and pride (at having helped to liberate so many pensioners from their imprisonment) as she led her motley crew down the steps of the building. Some had managed to find their outdoor clothes and were fully dressed. Others had slipped their coats over their pyjamas and nightdresses. And a few were still dressed in their dressing gowns and slippers. Fortunately, it was neither wet nor cold.

`You can't do this!' shouted Mr Fuller-Hawksmoor to their backs. `You come back here! Don't you think for one minute that you'll get away with this! I won't let you in when you come scurrying back wanting your rooms again!'

`Goodbye, and good riddance you nasty little man!' shouted Mrs Caldicot, over her shoulder.

`Goodbye, and good riddance you nasty little man!' shouted Miss Nightingale.

`Goodbye, and good riddance you nasty little man!' echoed Mrs Peterborough.

`Goodbye, and good riddance you nasty little man!' shouted the twelve other residents who were trooping along behind them.

***

Mrs Caldicot had formulated no clear plans for the future when she'd originally decided to leave The Twilight Years Rest Home. She had rather thought that she would just call a taxi, tell the driver to take her into town and then decide what to do next over a cup of coffee and a Danish pastry in the cafeteria on the top floor of the department store in the middle of town.

But telephoning for a taxi was now clearly impractical. (`I'd like a taxi, please.' `Where to?' `Into town.' `Certainly madam, how many passengers?' `Sixteen.' This did not have the ring of a conversation that was likely to prove profitable.) Mrs Caldicot also felt that her procession might be less than welcome in the department store cafeteria. She clearly had to make more immediate plans.

Half a mile down the road from The Twilight Years Rest Home Mrs Caldicot spotted the answer: a large hotel which specialised in catering for business executives.

Unhesitatingly, she led her procession of shuffling refugees through the car park, past the rows of Fords and Vauxhalls and BMWs, and into the lobby of the Mettleham Grand Hotel. A large group of besuited sales executives, about to start a meeting to launch a new breakfast cereal, were standing around in the lobby. They stared at Mrs Caldicot's procession. `It must be a marketing gimmick!' Mrs Caldicot heard one of them murmur.

`You sit down over there and wait for me!' Mrs Caldicot said firmly to Miss Nightingale, pointing to a group of luxurious, leather armchairs and sofas which were grouped around an artificial log fire.

`You sit down over there and wait for me!' said Mrs Peterborough firmly and much more loudly. She was, thought Mrs Caldicot, a useful aide-de-camp in these unusual circumstances.

Miss Nightingale and the rest of the procession shuffled over towards the cluster of leather chairs and sofas and obediently sat down while Mrs Caldicot, closely followed by the ever faithful Mrs Peterborough, headed for the reception desk.

`Can I help you, madam?' asked a rather startled looking young man, dressed in a dark suit and silver tie. He had a small brass name plate attached to his lapel but without her reading glasses Mrs Caldicot couldn't quite see what it said.

`I'd like some rooms, please,' said Mrs Caldicot. She put her handbag down on the reception counter.

`Some rooms, please!' echoed Mrs Peterborough. She put her kidney dish down on the reception counter next to Mrs Caldicot's handbag.

`How many rooms, madam?'

`Sixteen, please,' said Mrs Caldicot. `We'd like one each. All on the same floor.' She thought it would be a nice treat for everyone to have their own room for a change. Besides she didn't want to have to spend the rest of the day trying to work out who was going to share with whom.

`Sixteen, please,' said Mrs Peterborough.

`How long would that be for, madam?' asked the man on the reception desk, looking first at Mrs Caldicot and then at Mrs Peterborough and not knowing which to look at most. He glanced over towards the rest of the group.

`I'm not sure yet,' said Mrs Caldicot. `I'll let you know later on.'

`I'll let you know,' said Mrs Peterborough.

`Would it be possible to have a reduced rate?' asked Mrs Caldicot. `Since there are so many of us.'

`I beg your pardon, madam?' said the man on the reception desk, who genuinely hadn't heard.

`A reduced rate!' shouted Mrs Peterborough. `There are so many of us!'

`Of course, madam!' said the man on the reception desk apologetically. `Just one moment, please.' He scurried off to speak to the duty manager.

'I think they may be members of some strange religious group,' he whispered to the manager. 'Some of them seem to be wearing dressing gowns and nightdresses.'

'Saris perhaps?' suggested the manager, who was proud of his broadminded and non-racist attitudes. 'Maybe they're ethnic people?'

'I don't think they're ethnic,' said the man from the reception desk. 'But they want a reduced rate.'

'Then they must be O.K.,' said the manager. 'Jolly good. Put them on the twelfth floor.'

The man returned a moment later to the reception desk and smiled at Mrs Caldicot. 'No problem, madam,' he smiled. 'How will you be paying, madam?' he asked.

'I'll give you a cheque when we leave,' said Mrs Caldicot.

'Cheque.' said Mrs Peterborough firmly.

The man looked over the counter and, for the first time, saw Kitty. 'Is that a cat, madam?' he enquired.

'Probably,' said Mrs Caldicot. 'You don't charge extra for cats do you?'

'We don't allow cats at all, madam!' said the man sternly.

'I can't see any sign that says 'No Cats',' said Mrs Caldicot politely but firmly.

The receptionist pointed to a small black and white sign behind him which clearly said: 'No dogs allowed'.

'Do you think this is a dog?' asked Mrs Caldicot. 'Does she look like a dog to you?'

'No, madam,' said the man.

'Well, then,' said Mrs Caldicot. 'That's all right, isn't it?' And she and Miss Nightingale and Mrs Peterborough and all the rest of them went up to their rooms.

CHAPTER THIRTEEN

It was never really clear exactly who told the local television station about Mrs Caldicot's dramatic exodus from The Twilight Years Rest Home.

It was certainly not Mr Fuller-Hawksmoor.

He had spent the rest of that fateful day gloomily jabbing at his calculator with a podgy finger, trying to work out how he could possibly stay in business. Publicity was the last thing he wanted.

And it wasn't Mrs Caldicot either.

Prior to her time at The Twilight Years Rest Home she had always regarded the television set as something that was useful for standing flowers on. During her time at The Twilight Years Rest Home she had regarded the television set primarily as a sedative for Mrs Peterborough. She would have no more thought of telephoning the TV station than she would have thought of taking scuba diving lessons.

It could have been one of Mr Fuller-Hawksmoor's staff members, rejoicing in his discomfiture and anxious to share his discomfort with as wide an audience as possible; it may have been someone from the Mettleham Grand Hotel; or it might just have been someone who had seen Mrs Caldicot's straggling procession trooping along the roadway between The Twilight Years Rest Home and the hotel.

Anyway, it doesn't really matter who tipped off the television station. The fact is someone did and as a result that afternoon a whole television crew turned up at the Mettleham Grand Hotel and asked to speak to the leader of the group of elderly people who had booked into the hotel earlier that day.

***

By the time Mrs Caldicot had responded to the telephone call from the assistant deputy duty manager and had made her way downstairs, the camera crew had set up their equipment in the reception area and a man in the patterned sweater was re-arranging a vase of dried flowers so that they satisfied his acute sense of aesthetic perfection.

`Mrs Caldicot?' said a tall, statuesque blonde with piercing blue eyes, shoulder length hair and a smile that had persuaded politicians in all major parties to say far more than they had ever intended.

`What can I do for you?' asked Mrs Caldicot, nervously eyeing the camera crew.

`My name is Jacoranda Pettigrew. I'm a reporter from the local television station,' said the statuesque blonde, she indicated the chair that she wanted Mrs Caldicot to sit in.

`That's nice,' said Mrs Caldicot, obediently sitting down. Jacoranda, who wasn't easy to ignore or disappoint, sat down opposite her. As she settled herself down and waited for Jacoranda to speak Mrs Caldicot vividly remembered her last encounter with the media. It had been 55 years earlier. She had seen a milkman save a small girl from drowning in a local river. Despite the success of that meeting (which had resulted in her photograph appearing on page seven of her local newspaper) she was modest enough not to consider herself experienced in the matter of news interviews. She felt a frisson of uncertainty running up and down her spine.

`Will you talk to me for the camera?' asked Jacoranda, turning up her smile a couple of hundred watts.

`What on earth about?' asked Mrs Caldicot, guardedly.

`About where you and your friends have come from and what you're planning to do now,' replied Jacoranda, softly. `I know our viewers will be enthralled to hear what you have to say.' She could hear the sound engineer and the cameraman behind her adjusting their equipment and getting ready to start recording.

`Well, I don't know...' said Mrs Caldicot, uncertainly. `I've never done anything like this before.'

`You'll find that the sort of sympathetic publicity we can provide you with will be bound to help your cause,' said Jacoranda.

Mrs Caldicot, who hadn't really thought of herself as having a cause, couldn't help feeling that if she did turn out to have a cause then Jacoranda might well have a point. Anyway, she thought, surely the fact that she had never done anything like it before was a good reason for doing it now.

`O.K.,' she said, almost defiantly.

`That's wonderful!' murmured Jacoranda, patting Mrs Caldicot on the knee with a gesture which had in the past proved wonderfully effective when applied to the legs of middle aged men in grey suits. `Shall we start?' She turned and winked at the man in the patterned sweater who smiled back nervously and waved a hand telling the rest of the crew to start filming.

`Don't we have to rehearse?' asked Mrs Caldicot uncertainly.

`Not with you,' said Jacoranda, giving Mrs Caldicot another blast of her most dazzling smile. `I just know you're going to be absolutely wonderful!' She glanced briefly over her shoulder to make sure that the camera was running and then she asked her first question.

`Mrs Caldicot,' she said, `you arrived at the Mettleham Grand Hotel today at the head of a demonstration. Where did you come from?'

`I don't really know that you'd call it a demonstration,' said Mrs Caldicot. `But we've all come from `The Twilight Years Rest Home.'

`And you marched all the way here to protest?'

`I suppose it was more of a mass escape than a protest,' laughed Mrs Caldicot.

`Was that why so many of your fellow demonstrators were still in their dressing gowns and nightwear?'

`I suppose so,' nodded Mrs Caldicot. `We did come away in something of a hurry.'

`And why did you feel that you had to escape from The Twilight Years Rest Home?' asked Jacoranda.

`Well basically it was about Kitty,' said Mrs Caldicot.

`Kitty?' interrupted Jacoranda. `Is Kitty another of the demonstrators?'

`No. Kitty is my cat. Mr Fuller-Hawksmoor who runs the rest home said she couldn't stay and I thought she'd probably be taken to the vet's and put down so I decided to leave.'

`And all the other residents felt so strongly about it that they walked out in protest too?'

`I suppose that's right,' said Mrs Caldicot, who thought that if she tried to explain about Miss Nightingale and Mrs Peterborough the whole story might get too complicated. `Though I must admit that wasn't the start of it all,' she continued. `The trouble really began with the cabbage.'

`Tell me about the cabbage,' said Jacoranda, who knew already that this interview was going to be a winner. There was, she felt, something about Mrs Caldicot which would appeal to the ordinary viewer.

`Well, they used to give us horrible, smelly cabbage,' said Mrs Caldicot. `But Mr Fuller-Hawksmoor – he's the proprietor – got cross when I didn't want to eat it.'

Jacoranda, realising that she now had a wonderful story with which to end the evening news programme, leant forward. `So,' she said, momentarily inspired, `this is really a war about cabbage that you're fighting!'

`I suppose it is,' agreed Mrs Caldicot uncertainly.

`Have you had to leave any of your friends behind?' asked Jacoranda, her voice full of sadness.

`Well, yes,' said Mrs Caldicot. `The ones who were bedbound or stuck in wheelchairs couldn't come with us.'

`Thank you, Mrs Caldicot,' said Jacoranda. She turned round to face the camera. `This is Jacoranda Bartholomew with Mrs Caldicot, safely escaped from the cabbage wars at The Twilight Years Rest Home and now staying in a secret hideout, preparing to fight to help her friends join her in freedom.'

`Cut! Cut!' said the man in the patterned sweater, waving his arms about and looking very excited. He rushed over to the two of them. `Jacoranda, darling that was marvellous!' he said, giving the air next to her cheek a tremendous kiss. `Absolutely marvellous!' He turned to Mrs Caldicot. `We must have a few pictures of you and Kitty,' he said, clapping his hands together and looking coy. `And I want all your lovely friends to come down here into the lobby in their nightdresses and pyjamas and dressing gowns and whatnots!' He clapped his hands gleefully, like a small boy who has been told that he can play with the matches. `Oh this is such a lovely story!' he said. `Such a lovely story!'

The film crew spent the next thirty minutes shooting pictures of Mrs Caldicot with Kitty on her lap and with Kitty sitting beside her on the sofa. Then when they'd done that they spent another hour taking pictures of Mrs Caldicot, Miss Nightingale, Mrs Peterborough and all the rest of the escapees walking down the driveway to the hotel and then walking in through the lobby and filling both the lifts.

`Oh what a lovely story!' said the man in the patterned sweater when he had finished. He gave the air next to Mrs Caldicot's cheek a big kiss. `You're an absolute natural, darling!' he said. `Absolute natural, isn't she Jacoranda sweetheart?'

`Absolute natural,' agreed Jacoranda, giving the fortunate Mrs Caldicot a final chance to admire two neat and symmetrical rows of perfectly capped teeth.

CHAPTER FOURTEEN

`Mrs Caldicot's Cabbage Wars', as they quickly became known, immediately caught the public's imagination. Jacoranda Pettigrew's interview with Mrs Caldicot and the rest of The Twilight Years Rest Home refugees appeared on all that evening's news bulletins.

Within an hour of the first news programme finishing there was a queue of reporters from newspapers, magazines and radio stations waiting to talk to the woman who had led what one commentator had instantly and memorably called Britain's first `grey' revolution.

A man in a dark pinstripe suit who said he was from *The Sun*, a popular tabloid newspaper with a massive circulation, wanted to know Mrs Caldicot's twenty favourite non-cabbage recipes. A journalist in jeans and a sports jacket who wore his black hair slicked straight back and said he was from *The Times* wanted to know whether Mrs Caldicot thought that the use of cabbage was a socially divisive feature which only affected the economically deprived and was therefore a consequence of the advertising industry's obsession with youth. A girl in her early twenties who said that she was from *The Daily Mirror*, another tabloid newspaper, wanted to know whether or not Mrs Caldicot agreed that cabbage contained a variety of vitamins and minerals and was an excellent source of fibre. A lady feature writer who arrived dressed in a light grey suit and an Ascot hat and said she was from the *Daily Mail* wanted to know if Mrs Caldicot thought that her protest heralded the beginning of a major revolution among pensioners. A journalist in corduroy trousers and a jacket with leather patches on the elbows who said he was from a liberal newspaper called *The Guardian* was quite indignant about Mrs Caldicot's protest and wanted to know if Mrs Caldicot realised that according to his estimates the amount of cabbage wasted every day in British rest homes would feed the starving inhabitants of Somalia for a week. A girl journalist in a miniskirt and a baggy sweater who announced that she was from *The Independent* asked Mrs Caldicot whether she thought that the real blame for the problem lay with the farmers or the Economic Community's Common Agricultural Policy. A journalist in evening dress who apologetically explained that he had come from a dinner engagement and said he was from the *Financial Times* wanted to know if Mrs Caldicot realised that by her action she had threatened a major British industry. And a journalist in a grubby mackintosh from the *Daily Sport* wanted to know if Mrs Caldicot had any granddaughters who would be prepared to be photographed without any clothes on. A reporter from the local paper wanted to know how Mrs Caldicot's age, how long she had lived in the area and the names and addresses of all her relatives.

All of these reporters arrived with their own photographers in tow and Mrs Caldicot rapidly grew tired of posing either with Kitty or with Miss Nightingale and Mrs Peterborough.

But, despite all this press interest, it was undoubtedly the call from the researcher asking if Mrs Caldicot would appear on the Mike Trickle Television Chat Show the following evening which promised to turn her into a real celebrity. The appearance on the Mike Trickle Television Chat Show was, however, still twenty four hours away and Mrs Caldicot had other more immediately pressing problems to face.

***

At half past ten that evening, having watched herself on television for the third time and having dealt with all the reporters, Mrs Caldicot decided that she would pop in to see what the others thought of it all, and to check that they were all safely tucked up for the night.

Miss Nightingale hadn't seen the programme because she hadn't yet bothered to turn on her television set. She had, however, discovered the joys of room service and every flat surface in the room held a tray which was positively groaning with expensive looking delicacies.

'Look!' said Miss Nightingale, who had been unable to hide a temporary look of disappointment when she had opened the door to her room to find Mrs Caldicot instead of a waiter standing there, was soon excitedly taking Mrs Caldicot on a tour of her collection of delicacies.

There were: scrambled eggs on toast, a pot of Earl Grey tea with lemon, buttered crumpets and toast set on trays on top of the low coffee table in front of the sofa; fresh scones served with dairy cream and strawberry jam on a bedside table; egg and cress sandwiches, a bottle of claret with two glasses, chicken salad sandwiches, a pot of fresh coffee and a fresh melon on the writing table; thinly sliced fresh salmon with brown bread, a bottle of champagne in an ice bucket and pancakes with lemon and sugar on top of the television set; boiled eggs with fingers of toast, a double whisky, battered scampi and vegetable soup with croutons on trays on the bed; and a plateful of Danish pastries, a bottle of Taylor's vintage port, a dish of garlic bread and a plateful of spaghetti bolognaise on trays beside the sink in the bathroom.

`What on earth have you been doing?' asked Mrs Caldicot, horrified, when she all the food and drink that Miss Nightingale had ordered. Before Miss Nightingale could answer there was a loud knock on the bedroom door. Miss Nightingale hurried to answer it and moments later admitted a tall young man in a white coat who walked into the room carrying a large tray which he put down onto the bed next to the trays carrying the boiled eggs, the whisky, the scampi and the soup. He smiled broadly at Miss Nightingale and handed her a pad to sign. Then he thanked her, bowed very slightly and let himself out.

`Isn't it wonderful?' asked Miss Nightingale, excitedly, when he had gone. `I just pick up the telephone and tell them what they want and then POOF, like magic...' she waved her hands to indicate how easy it was to make the food appear.

`But all this food will cost a fortune!' protested Mrs Caldicot, looking around in horror.

`It doesn't cost anything!' insisted Miss Nightingale. `I didn't have to give them any money at all!' She leant forwards confidentially, `The young men bring it because they like me,' she whispered, `I think I must be famous because they all want my autograph!' She stopped and thought. `I don't remember why I'm famous,' she added. For a brief moment she looked thoughtful and slightly puzzled but this sign of confusion soon passed and was replaced by a smile.

Miss Nightingale was so excited by it all that Mrs Caldicot didn't have the heart to tell her off, or even to tell her that she mustn't order any more food from room service. As Mrs Caldicot left, Miss Nightingale picked up the telephone again and, using the extensive room service menu, began ordering a fresh seafood platter with brown bread and butter and a side order of French fries.

Mrs Peterborough in the room next door had not yet discovered the joys of room service but she had found out how to operate the television set.

After she had let Mrs Caldicot in, she rushed back into her room and sat down on the floor about two feet away from the set. She then had an increasingly agitated time as she watched a series of advertisements. (Mrs Caldicot usually switched over when the advertisements came on because she knew that their brevity and content confused Mrs Peterborough enormously. She had once watched her friend collapse in despair as she struggled to adopt the personality of a talking lavatory seat).

`I wouldn't swap my one packet of New Dazzle washing powder for two packets of my old powder,' said a pretty young actress, hugging a box of New Dazzle soap powder to her chest as though it were an expensive string of pearls.

`I wouldn't swap my one packet of New Dazzle washing powder,' promised Mrs Peterborough, hugging an imaginary box of soap powder to her chest. `I wouldn't!' she insisted. `No I wouldn't!' She looked across at Mrs Caldicot. `I wouldn't!' she promised.

`I know you wouldn't,' said Mrs Caldicot softly.

`You'll get a home not a house when you buy from Sherlock Homes!' said a fat man in a tightly fitting grey suit, holding his arms out wide. He was standing in the middle of a small, brand new housing estate and looking up at the camera which was clearly being operated from a helicopter high overhead. `And don't forget,' he shouted, as the helicopter hurtled skywards, `free carpets, free curtains and the best mortgage rate you can find!'

`A home not a house! Free carpets, free curtains and the best mortgage rate!' shouted Mrs Peterborough, struggling to match his enthusiasm. `The best mortgage rate you can find!' she cried, clearly overtaken by the excitement of it all. She peered at the television set, apparently looking for the salesman.

But he'd gone.

`I hate new Germ-o-blast,' muttered an evil sounding, slimy looking cartoon germ. The germ scowled as a woman carrying a plastic bottle of disinfectant approached. `Grrrrr!' said the germ, trying to hide under the rim of a lavatory bowl.

Mrs Peterborough shuddered in distaste. `I hate new Germ-o-blast!' she said, screwing up her mouth as though she'd been sucking a lemon. `Grrrrr!'

The woman took the top off her bottle and squirted a few ounces into the lavatory bowl.

`Aaaaargh!' screamed the cartoon germ. `This is the end for me!'

Mrs Peterborough screamed too and held her hands up to her face in horror.

Mrs Caldicot leant forward and switched to another channel. A beautiful young couple were making love in a wood.

`Oh, darling!' said the girl.

`Darling!' said the man.

`Oh, darling!' said Mrs Peterborough, the agony of a moment ago now forgotten and replaced by a look of tenderness and affection.

Mrs Caldicot tiptoed out of the room and left the three of them to enjoy their romance. She couldn't help wishing for just a moment that she could forget her worries and her sorrows as easily as Mrs Peterborough could.

CHAPTER FIFTEEN

`Here comes Mike,' murmured Sally, the researcher, to Mrs Caldicot. They were sitting together in the rather grubby waiting room which the receptionist had rather grandly and misleadingly referred to as `The Green Room'. A scattered jumble of stiffening sandwiches were strewn over two large plates on a low table in the centre of the room and a coffee percolator spluttered and hissed on a metal trolley. A huge television set dominated the room.

The name of the room was misleading for the walls were painted blue, the furniture was brown and although the carpet was heavily patterned there was no green to be seen in it anywhere. The only thing in the room that was green was a modern, plastic telephone on a small wooden table by the door. It was, thought Mrs Caldicot, rather strange to name a room after the colour of a telephone. `Don't be nervous!' added Sally, a pretty young thing in her early twenties. She wore a pale lilac skirt and a white blouse, carried a huge sheaf of notes in a large cardboard folder and seemed desperately in need of her own advice. Mrs Caldicot thought Sally was probably the most nervous person she had ever met. `He's awfully nice!' Sally whispered with a shiver. Mrs Caldicot, who had been collected from the Mettleham Grand Hotel by taxi and told that she had to arrive at the studios three hours before `The Mike Trickle Chat Show' was due to start, was now very, very bored. She was fed up with talking to the researcher. Sally seemed to think that Mrs Caldicot was interested only in talking about nursing homes or listening to her boring anecdotes about the old people she had known. She was fed up with watching the endless stream of cameramen, soundmen and production assistants sneaking into the room to steal the sandwiches (a packet of chocolate biscuits which a white-coated canteen assistant had brought with the sandwiches had been broken into and distributed amongst the technicians within seconds of their arrival), and she was very fed up with watching the endless rehearsals for the evening's programme.

`Mike,' said Sally, clearly impressed by the presence of the great man and assuming that Mrs Caldicot would be too, `this is Mrs

Caldicot.' She didn't do the introduction the other way round, clearly assuming that Mrs Caldicot would know who Mike Trickle was.

This was, of course, true for although Mrs Caldicot had never heard of Mike Trickle before the previous evening she had watched him carefully rehearsing his ad-libs for the worst part of three hours. Nevertheless, she could hardly believe that this was the same person.

The Mike Trickle whom she had been watching on the television had seemed urbane, relaxed, witty and handsome. But this Mike Trickle, the real one, was nervous and clearly agitated. He looked bad tempered and his smooth, healthy, slightly suntanned complexion had clearly come out of a jar; a very large jar thought Mrs Caldicot looking at the thick layer of cream which covered the TV star's cheeks and forehead. He was much shorter than he looked on the television screen and he had the worst case of halitosis that Mrs Caldicot had ever encountered. It was his hair which Mrs Caldicot found herself most fascinated by. The hair which had looked healthy and natural on the television screen now looked as healthy and as natural as a scouring pad. A new scouring pad, but nevertheless a scouring pad.

`Hello!' said Mike Trickle, briefly turning on his smile. He was accompanied by a pneumatic blonde who seemed to have been grafted or glued onto his arm. `It's great to have you on the programme. You had good cuttings this morning.' He turned the smile off as though to save the batteries.

`Nice to meet you,' said Mrs Caldicot, having difficulty in dragging her eyes away from the awful wig the man was wearing and wondering why no one told him how silly he looked. She hadn't yet got round to reading the morning's newspapers though Mike Trickle wasn't the first person to tell her that her story had appeared in them. `I've seen you on there,' she said, nodding towards the television monitor in the corner of the room. Mr Trickle did not realise that Mrs Caldicot was speaking literally but naturally assumed that she meant that she was a long time fan. In recognition of this he gave her another fifteen second burst of the smile. The blonde's smile seemed wired up to Mr Trickle's for when he smiled she smiled too. When he stopped smiling she stopped smiling. Mrs Caldicot suddenly noticed that the TV star also had what looked like a hearing aid in his right ear.

`It'll all be very straightforward,' said Mr Trickle, reassuringly.

`I'll ask you about the cabbage and you just tell me what happened.'
He seemed to think about smiling for a moment then changed his
mind. He turned to Sally. `Have the Vandals turned up yet?' he asked
her.

`I don't think so, Mike,' said Sally, apologetically. `I'll check with
Peter.' She hurried off across the room towards the telephone.

`Damned pop group,' said Mike to Mrs Caldicot. `Have you heard
of them?'

`Is it Vandals with a capital V?' asked Mrs Caldicot, speaking
rather more loudly than usual, and as clearly as she could, so that the
deaf celebrity could understand her.

`Yes. I suppose so,' replied Mike, instinctively moving his head
backwards a few inches and wondering why Mrs Caldicot had
suddenly started shouting.

`Then I don't think so,' said Mrs Caldicot, enunciating carefully in
case Mr Trickle relied on lip reading.

`They've had two hits and of course they think they're superstars
now,' said Mike. He decided that the old woman was probably batty.
Accompanied by the sticky blonde he strode off towards the remains
of the sandwiches, flicked through them as though leafing through
the magazines in a dentist's waiting room and then slipped what
looked like a piece of ham into his mouth. Sally put the telephone
down, walked back across the room and said something to him.
Mike didn't answer but just strode off angrily. The blonde's stiletto
heels click clacked furiously on the corridor floor as she struggled to
keep up with him.

`It's a shame about him being deaf,' said Mrs Caldicot when Sally
returned faithfully to her side. It was clearly her job to keep Mrs
Caldicot entertained.

`Deaf?' said Sally, puzzled.

`Mrs Caldicot leant towards her. `I saw the deaf aid,' she
whispered.

`Oh!' laughed Sally, nervously. `That isn't a deaf aid. It's a tiny
radio so that the director can talk to him.'

`Ah!' whispered Mrs Caldicot, nodding to show that she
understood though she still didn't really understand why the director
would want to talk to Mr Trickle while he was broadcasting. `And
why doesn't his wife tell him not to wear that silly wig?'

`The wig?' said Sally, blanching and looking behind her to make sure that no one was listening.

'It's not a very good one, is it?' said Mrs Caldicot.

'Sshhh!' said Sally, holding a finger to her lips. 'It's a big secret. How did you know about the wig?'

'I'd have to be blind not to know!' laughed Mrs Caldicot. 'I've seen more convincing hair on a toothbrush.''And that's not his wife,' added Sally, looking around to make sure that no one was listening. Since apart from Mrs Caldicot and herself the only other occupants of the room were the sandwiches her fears were unfounded.

***

Thirty minutes later Sally took Mrs Caldicot into the make- up department where a nice young lady with a lot of frizzy red hair filled in her wrinkles, livened up her eyebrows and painted her lips a rather ferocious shade of red.

Then Sally took Mrs Caldicot along to the studio where she wished her all the very best of luck and handed her over to a girl in blue jeans and a T-shirt who wore a pair of headphones with a microphone attached and who introduced herself as Jenny. Jenny took Mrs Caldicot behind a large piece of painted scenery where the floor was covered with huge thick cables and told her to wait there and to be quiet. A voice suddenly crackled faintly in the headphones she was wearing and Jenny apologised and hurried off. Mrs Caldicot peered around the edge of the scenery and could see a small audience sitting quietly in their seats waiting for the show to start. She wondered how long they'd had to wait and then she realised that she wanted to spend a penny.

She retraced her steps, said 'Hello!' to three men in jeans and plaid shirts, slipped out through a door marked 'Exit' and found herself in a corridor which she didn't recognise and which seemed to stretch forever and ever. She walked down it for a minute or so, passing several doorways on her way, and eventually found a door marked Ladies.

When she came out a minute or two later she couldn't remember which way she'd come so she followed her instincts and turned left. After she had walked for another hundred yards she realised that she had gone the wrong way and so she turned right when she saw an illuminated sign which said Studio.

When she got to the studio she opened the door cautiously. The room was deserted and was clearly not the one she had left a few moments earlier. She intended to retrace her steps but once again she took the wrong turning and quickly realised that she was well and truly lost.

Mrs Caldicot decided that if she kept walking she would be bound to find someone who could help her find her way back to the right studios and so she continued her journey around the labyrinth of corridors.

`Excuse me!' she said, politely to a man who was wearing a dark blue uniform and had the word Security printed on his chest and his hat. He seemed to be guarding a door.

`What are you doing there?' demanded the man, rather aggressively.

`I'm lost,' said Mrs Caldicot. `Can you tell me how I find the studio where the Mike Trickle show is being broadcast from?'

The security guard frowned and looked at his watch. `It's due to go live on air in three minutes,' he said. `I think you're probably too late now.'

`Oh dear,' said Mrs Caldicot. `What a pity.'

`Go out through this door,' said the guard, relenting and feeling sorry for her. `Walk along the street for two hundred yards and you'll come to the main entrance. They may just let you slip in at the back of the audience.'

Mrs Caldicot followed his instructions and walked along the street to the main entrance. `Hello!' she said to the man guarding the main entrance. `Can you tell me how to get to the studio where they are broadcasting the Mike Trickle show?'

The security guard shook his head and sucked air in through his teeth. `I think you've missed it, love,' he said, sadly. He looked at his watch. He examined a list of names in front of him. `What's your name?'

`Mrs Caldicot,' replied Mrs Caldicot.

The guard looked up. `Thelma Caldicot?'

`Yes!' smiled Mrs Caldicot.

`Oh my God!' said the guard. `They're going mad up there looking for you! Where have you been?' He picked up a telephone and dialled a three digit number. `She's here!' he said. `Yes! Mrs Caldicot.' He listened for a moment and then put the telephone down. `Wait here!' he said. He came out of his cubicle, lifted a large key from a ring on his belt and locked the entrance door so that no one could sneak in while he was gone and then headed off into the depths of the building. `Follow me!' he cried over his shoulder. Hurrying was not a form of motion which came easy to him and he swayed a little from side to side as his stability came under threat from his speed.

Half a minute later they met Sally running towards them. She had been crying and had mascara all over her cheeks. Behind Sally ran a man in a sports coat and a woman in a blue suit. They were both shouting hysterically. `Where have you been?' and `We're on air in thirty seconds!' were the only two things Mrs Caldicot could decipher from their gibbering.

They quickly escorted her back to the studio and deposited her once more behind the painted scenery. Mike Trickle was just being given an enthusiastic welcome by the audience.

`Where have you been?' hissed a harassed looking Jenny. `You're on!' she said, and without more ado she pushed Mrs Caldicot from behind the scenery and out into the bright lights of the studio.

Mrs Caldicot was live on national television.

***

`Welcome to the Mike Trickle Show!' said Mike Trickle, giving Mrs Caldicot one of his most incandescent smiles. Mrs Caldicot could see that he was sweating heavily. Something seemed to have been worrying him for he had developed a small twitch in the muscles around his left eye.

The audience, encouraged by a small, fat man who was holding up a large placard, clapped enthusiastically. Mrs Caldicot wondered what the placard said. She couldn't read it because it was facing the wrong way. The small, fat man, who had sweat stains on the back of his T-shirt and underneath his armpits, lowered his sign and the clapping stopped instantly. Mrs Caldicot could now see that the placard bore the single word `CLAP' in large red letters.

`Mrs Caldicot,' said Mike Trickle, `you're in the news at the moment because you led a walk out among residents at The Twilight Years Rest Home. It is believed to be the first walk out of its kind ever to take place in this country. Do you think your action will herald the beginning of a revolution among older citizens?'

Mrs Caldicot stared at him and found that she had difficulty in concentrating. She could not take her eyes off his wig which, she suddenly realised, looked rather like a sleeping kitten curled up on top of a turnip.

`I don't know,' she said, honestly and simply. There was a silence which Trickle waited, in vain, for Mrs Caldicot to fill. The silence was broken only by a buzz from an audience which had never before heard anyone confess their ignorance on prime time television.

`You don't know!' said Trickle to his guest. He spoke in a mocking sort of voice, rather like a stern parent quizzing a stubborn child.

`Sometimes life isn't so much about knowing the answers as about knowing the right questions to ask,' said Mrs Caldicot simply. When she had spoken she hoped that Mr Trickle didn't take offence. She had meant none. The audience, which would have taken against her if they had suspected that she was trying to be clever, recognised her simple honesty and a few of them instinctively took her to their collective bosom.

Mike Trickle should have been warned. But he was too stupid to realise the danger. He glanced down at the next question on the piece of paper on his lap. `You claim that you led the walk out simply because you don't like cabbage. Don't you think that was selfish and irresponsible of you? Wasn't it a rather dramatic response to a childish dislike of cabbage?'

`That's not what happened at all,' said Mrs Caldicot, rather hurt and indignant. `It's true that I walked out of the dining room because I didn't want to eat any more cabbage but that wasn't why I left the rest home, and it certainly wasn't why any of the others left the home. I left the dining room because I thought the cabbage smelt horrid but that is only one small part of the story.'

`That's a rather small reason for such a big deed isn't it?' said Mike Trickle. `If everyone walked out because of one pungent vegetable the world would be a pretty turbulent place, wouldn't it? Isn't it true, as some people are saying, that you led the walk out simply to draw attention to yourself?'

Mrs Caldicot stared at him for a moment as though she couldn't quite believe what she had heard. `That's rather rude of you,' she said. `Why are you being so aggressive? I didn't want to attract attention to myself at all.'

`Oh, come on now!' said Mr Trickle. `You're here on national television aren't you?'

`But only because you asked me to come,' said Mrs Caldicot. `And to be honest with you I'm beginning to wish I hadn't come. There's a rather good old black and white film on the other side that I'd have quite liked to watch.'

The audience laughed spontaneously. Out of the corner of her eye Mrs Caldicot could see that the fat man was waving his hands horizontally in an attempt to quell the spirited response.

`But some people might argue that by leading a walk out you've endangered the lives of many old people,' persisted Mike Trickle, who was desperate to enhance his reputation as a tough current affairs presenter and to get rid of his light and frothy showbiz image. `Isn't it true that some of the old people who left with you are in their seventies and eighties?'

`Yes,' agreed Mrs Caldicot. `But just because people are old that doesn't mean that they can't make their own minds up. Just because people are eighty they don't have to put up with things that younger people wouldn't put up with. Why do you young people feel you have a right to sneer and snigger at us old folk?'

`I haven't heard of many thirty-year-olds leaving home because they didn't like the smell of the cabbage,' said Trickle. After making sure that the camera wasn't on him he turned towards the audience and pulled a face, mocking Mrs Caldicot.

`It wasn't like that,' insisted Mrs Caldicot. `It was more about my cat than the cabbage.' She explained what Mr Fuller-Hawksmoor had said about Kitty.

`So all these people, in their nightwear, walked out into the cold because of your cat?'

`I didn't ask them to come with me,' said Mrs Caldicot. `They all just followed me.'

Mike Trickle, deciding that he was on safe ground with an old lady with no previous television experience, leant back, abandoned his scripted questions and bravely ad-libbed.

`Are you seriously claiming that you are so charismatic that all these people just followed you?' he asked, sarcastically. He turned to the audience and pulled a disbelieving face. There was a faint and rather hollow splutter of laughter. Most of it came from technicians and researchers.

'No,' said Mrs Caldicot firmly but quietly. 'I'm just telling you what happened. Why are you determined to be so rude to me? Why do you keep making faces to the audience? How would you like it if I asked you why you wore such a silly wig or whether your wife knows about that blonde girl who was glued to your arm earlier on?'

Mike Trickle, who was so touchy and self-conscious about his hair piece that he had threatened to sue every newspaper which had ever dared even to suggest that his hair wasn't entirely his own, paled and opened his mouth to reply. All that came out was a rather faint 'What did you say?' He was still trying to work out whether or not Mrs Caldicot really had mentioned his wife.

'How would you like it if I asked you why you wore such a silly wig?' asked Mrs Caldicot, repeating her question. 'And have your wife and that blonde girl you were with been introduced to each another?' She spoke clearly and deliberately as though addressing someone hard of hearing. She still didn't entirely believe the explanation that Sally had given her for the hearing aid Mike Trickle wore.

Mike Trickle tried to respond but even if he had managed to get any words out no one would have heard them. The audience erupted and the sound of laughter and cheering would have drowned a brass band. The director went into an advertising break nine minutes early and Jenny, red-faced and looking desperate, rushed out and dragged Mrs Caldicot out of her chair.

Mrs Caldicot's moment of glory on 'The Mike Trickle Show' was over.

But Mrs Caldicot's moment of glory was, in reality, only just beginning.

CHAPTER SIXTEEN

Overnight Mrs Caldicot became a national celebrity.

Previously, much of the emphasis had been on what she had done, but now the emphasis was on who she was. Feature writers telephoned to say that their editors wanted them to write profiles of her. Radio producers wanted her to choose her favourite records and give her views on both national and international politics. Mrs Caldicot had become a woman of some importance.

The morning after her appearance on `The Mike Trickle Chat Show' Mrs Caldicot was the star guest on the nation's biggest and most successful television breakfast programme; pushing the previously booked guest, a mediocre politician who had acquired some temporary notoriety by introducing a bill to increase taxes, out of the programme schedule completely.

`I don't know,' said Mrs Caldicot, reluctantly, to the television researcher who telephoned her to ask her to appear on their programme. `I was hoping to spend some time trying to find somewhere cheaper to stay.'

`Oh don't worry about your hotel bill,' said the girl researcher. `We'll pay that.' The researcher was already hugging herself because she reckoned that she could get Mrs Caldicot to agree to appear for a fee of £25 which was a tenth of the amount she knew that the producer would have paid.

`All of it? Everything that's on my bill?' said Mrs Caldicot, genuinely surprised.

`Everything!' agreed the researcher, as a faint twinge of anxiety disturbed her equilibrium and as she quietly wondered just how much room service one old lady could possibly use.

`Wonderful!' said Mrs Caldicot, not bothering the researcher with the information that the accounts for all sixteen rooms, including Miss Nightingale's, were all being put on her bill.

The breakfast programme didn't want its guests there quite so long before the start of the programme. A chauffeur driven limousine picked Mrs Caldicot up from her hotel at 5.30 am. She arrived at the studio entrance at 6.00 am and was on air, made up and clutching a plastic beaker of coffee at 6.15 am.

'Welcome to the Breakfast Show,' said the presenter, a portly, cheery man who looked uncomfortable in a pair of grey slacks and a pink sweater. He had cut his teeth as a foreign correspondent and was now given all of the programmes 'big name' interviews. The presenter, whose real name was Cyril worked under the professional name of Peter. His colleague, whose real name was Flora-May but who called herself Susie, sat back in her chair, well out of camera shot, and studied the notes for her interview with a man who had trained a hedgehog to walk a miniature tightrope.

Mrs Caldicot, sitting next to Peter on a hideous and uncomfortably soft pink sofa, smiled and thanked him very much.

'Before we go any further,' said the presenter, smiling, 'I want to make it quite clear that this is all my own!' He reached up and lightly patted his neatly coiffed hair. The girl from the make-up department who had spent twenty minutes washing, combing, cutting and applying several layers of lacquer to his locks blanched off camera and relaxed only when his hand moved away. He turned and winked at the camera as the producer and he had agreed he would.

'That's nice,' said Mrs Caldicot, who instinctively felt that she didn't like Peter very much.

'We tried to get Mike Trickle to come onto the programme with you,' said Peter the presenter. 'But his agent told us that he's resting and our contact at 'The Mike Trickle Chat Show' tells us that Jack Burgess, Mike's stand in, will be taking over the show for a while.'

He spoke of their 'contact' as though getting information from 'The Mike Trickle Chat Show' was more difficult than getting information out of MI5, which, indeed, it quite probably was.

'Oh, dear,' said Mrs Caldicot. 'How sad. I do hope Mr Trickle isn't too poorly.'

'Just a badly dented pride, I suspect,' sniggered the breakfast presenter. Mrs Caldicot decided that she didn't like Peter at all. He picked up his notes. 'Now, tell me, Mrs Caldicot,' he said, 'did you decide before you went onto the programme what you were going to say to Mike?' Peter leant forwards, as though speaking confidentially, 'Did someone put you up to it?' he asked.

Mrs Caldicot felt and looked puzzled. 'How could I decide beforehand what I was going to say?' she asked. 'I didn't know what he was going to say!'

`And no one else put you up to it?'

`Of course not!' said Mrs Caldicot, rather indignantly. `Why would they?' She wondered if television people always asked their guests such impertinent questions. Asking if she had allowed herself to be told what to say by someone else suggested that she didn't have a mind of her own. Still, she thought, maybe people on television programmes were always supposed to be rude to one another. She decided that she wasn't going to be rude, however. She thought that she would ask a perfectly innocuous question to try to change the topic. She leant across the sofa, `Excuse me for asking,' she said, `but is that a deaf aid you're wearing or is it true that you wear it so that other people can tell you what to say and what to do?' She pointed towards the ear piece that the presenter was wearing.

`No, no!' laughed the presenter, automatically fingering his ear piece. `That's just so that the director can talk to me.'

`While you're talking to me?'

`Yes!' replied Peter, looking down at his list of questions to try to find his place.

`Isn't that rather rude?' asked Mrs Caldicot. `Him whispering to you while you're talking to me? If I wore one of those and I had people talking to me you'd think me rather odd wouldn't you?'

`He doesn't talk to me all the time,' said the presenter, rather defensively. `Just if there's something he wants me to ask you.'

`Find the hedgehog man!' shouted the director in the control room to his assistant.

Mrs Caldicot frowned. `Can't you think of your own questions?'

The presenter fingered his earpiece very nervously. `Yes, of course I can!' he laughed.

`Well, doesn't the director trust you then?' asked Mrs Caldicot.

Peter swallowed and then cleared his throat. `I'm sure he does,' he said. He turned to the camera and smiled, a favourite and usually successful trick of his. He always used it when things weren't going well. But this time it was a thin, rather wan smile and the discomfort showed through. The director said something to Peter but he didn't catch it and so he pressed on his ear piece with the forefinger of his right hand.

`Can't see the hedgehog man anywhere,' hissed the floor manager into his two way radio. Susie who was listening to this conversation on her ear piece looked around her, desperately searching for someone she could talk to about tightrope walking hedgehogs.

`Is he talking to you now?' asked Mrs Caldicot.

`Er...yes,' said the presenter, still struggling to hear what was being said to him.

`Ask the silly old bag what she and the other daft beggars are going to do next?' shouted the director. `Ask her where they're going!'

`What's he saying?' persisted Mrs Caldicot.

`Er...he wants me to ask you what you and your fellow escapees are going to do next?' The presenter was now sweating profusely and hoping desperately that he wasn't shaking visibly.

`Then why doesn't he come into the studio and ask me himself?' asked Mrs Caldicot. `Why does he have to ask you to ask me?'

The presenter, now entirely defeated, just shrugged.

`This television business all seems very silly to me,' said Mrs Caldicot, firmly.

The director, deciding to abandon Peter and to give up on the man with the clever hedgehog, was also sweating profusely. He screamed urgent instructions at the resident cook who, caught completely unawares, threw her furtive and completely illicit cigarette down onto the floor, turned to her nearest camera and smiled broadly. `Welcome, to Cook's Corner,' she read from the autocue, `this morning I'm going to show you how to boil an egg and make toast soldiers!'

Twenty seconds later, as one researcher hurried Mrs Caldicot out of the studio and a second struggled to compose the shattered presenter on the pink sofa and a third gave Susie, who was having an attack of wheezing, a glass of water, the smouldering cigarette abandoned by the cook triggered the sprinkler system and the whole studio was turned into a gigantic and very expensive shower room.

The director replaced the rest of the programme with cartoons and then got onto the telephone immediately to ask his agent to see if the job making corporate videos was still available.

CHAPTER SEVENTEEN

Mrs Caldicot was becoming a real celebrity. It seemed that everyone in the world wanted to take photographs of her or to interview her. Mrs Caldicot, however, had other, more important things on her mind.

It was comforting to know that the breakfast television company had agreed to pay the hotel bill but Mrs Caldicot still had no idea what she and her friends were going to do next.

She had just got back to the Mettleham Grand Hotel and was about to set off to catch the bus into the town to try to find somewhere cheaper for them all to stay when the telephone in her room started to ring. She picked it up reluctantly, half expecting to find a reporter on the other end. But it wasn't a reporter, it was one of the hotel receptionists.

`I'm sorry to bother you, Mrs Caldicot,' said the receptionist respectfully. `But I've got a man here who says he's your son.'

`Derek?' said Mrs Caldicot, questioningly.

She heard the receptionist repeat the name to someone. There was a brief pause. `Yes, that's right,' said the receptionist, a moment later. `He's here with a lady and a young man.'

`That'll be Derek,' sighed Mrs Caldicot. `Tell him I'm coming down and I'll meet him in the lobby.'

***

`Really, mother, I don't know what to say!' said Derek.

The four of them were sitting together in a corner of the lounge and Mrs Caldicot ordered a pot of tea for three and a cola drink. Jason was reading a computer magazine, listening to tinny noises on his headphones and surreptitiously squeezing a spot. `I have never been so embarrassed in the whole of my life,' Derek continued.

`I've always been a great fan of Mike Trickle's,' said Veronica. She spoke quietly as though frightened that someone might overhear. She was wearing a bright yellow trouser suit and lime green shoes. `How could you do that to him?'

`We put a lot of effort into finding you a really nice home,' said Derek. `A lot of effort.'

`And this is how you repay us!' said Veronica. `That poor Mr Trickle. They say he's had a nervous breakdown! I'll never forgive you if that quiz programme of his doesn't come back.'

`No you didn't!' said Mrs Caldicot, speaking to her son. `The Twilight Years Rest Home was the only place we visited!'

`Now, please, mother!' said Derek, wearily. `I don't know what's got into you recently. Don't start arguing and being clever with me. The Twilight Years Rest Home is a very widely respected institution and Mr Fuller-Hawksmoor does a splendid job.'

`No it's not,' said Mrs Caldicot firmly. `It's a terrible place and Mr Fuller-Hawksmoor is a tyrant.'

An elderly couple who had been standing a few yards away staring wandered over and stopped next to Mrs Caldicot. The man coughed.

`Yes?' said Veronica, rather shortly. `Can we help you?'

`Are you Mrs Caldicot?' asked the man, speaking to Mrs Caldicot. Mrs Caldicot said she was.

`Can I just shake your hand,' said the man. `I think you've taken a magnificent stand! I want to congratulate you and to wish you all the very best in your fight.' He held his hand out tentatively. Mrs Caldicot took it and shook it. The man beamed with delight. `We have no one else to fight for us,' he said quietly.

`We saw you on the television this morning,' said the woman. `You were marvellous.' Mrs Caldicot shook her hand too.

`That's very kind of you,' said Mrs Caldicot, who was rather overwhelmed by it all.

The elderly couple smiled a lot and backed away as though leaving the presence of royalty.

`You were on again this morning?' hissed Veronica, leaning forward in her chair and scowling at Mrs Caldicot.

`Yes.'

`Which programme?'

`I was on one of those breakfast programmes,' said Mrs Caldicot. `I can't remember which one. I never watch any of them.'

`Well I just hope you were better behaved this time,' said Veronica, leaning back and clasping her hands in her lap as though to say that she knew very well that Mrs Caldicot would not have behaved any better at all.

'This can't go on, mother,' said Derek, very firmly. 'You're making yourself a laughing stock.'

'Not to mention us,' added Veronica. 'Though I don't suppose you think of us.'

'And how on earth are you expecting to pay for this hotel?' asked Derek.

'I'm glad you've got the money,' said Veronica, sarcastically. She looked around. 'I'm sure that Derek and I wouldn't be able to afford to stay here.'

Just then the waiter returned with a tray. He put it down on the table in front of Mrs Caldicot. 'Is that all, Mrs Caldicot?' he asked.

Mrs Caldicot smiled at him. 'Thank you, yes,' she said. She took the proffered pen and bar statement and signed the latter with the former.

'Excuse me,' said a woman of about thirty five who had appeared as if from nowhere. 'I'm sorry to bother you,' she apologised, 'but could my daughters have your autograph? They saw you on the television.' Her two daughters, aged about nine or ten, appeared shyly from behind her back.

'Well,' said Mrs Caldicot, embarrassed. 'I don't know...'

'Oh, please do,' said the woman. 'I know it must be inconvenient being asked for your autograph all the time...'

'Have you got a piece of paper?' asked Mrs Caldicot.

The woman offered Mrs Caldicot a piece of Mettleham Grand Hotel stationery which she had obviously picked up from one of the writing tables.

'Do you have a pen?' asked Mrs Caldicot.

The woman rummaged in her handbag and handed Mrs Caldicot a pen. Mrs Caldicot put the notepaper down on the table, signed her name twice, once for each daughter, and then handed the notepaper and the pen back to the woman.

'Oh thank you!' said the woman, examining the signatures. She hurried her two daughters away.

'Well! Really!' said Veronica. 'I've never seen anything like it! Behaving like a film star!' she turned to her husband. 'Are you going to say anything to her?' she asked him.

'It's got to stop, mother,' said Derek. 'I think we'd better take you back to The Twilight Years Rest Home.' He paused. 'If you apologise I'm sure that Mr Fuller-Hawksmoor will take you back.'

Mrs Caldicot stared at him in astonishment. `Why on earth should I apologise?' she asked him, genuinely puzzled.

`Come on now, mother,' sighed Derek, as though running out of patience, `you've said some terrible things about him.'

`I've only told the truth,' protested Mrs Caldicot, wondering why honesty, which she had always thought of as a virtue, had suddenly come to be regarded as a sin. `Why on earth is everyone so frightened of the truth?'

`I'm sorry to bother you, Mrs Caldicot,' said one of the assistant managers, quietly. None of them had seen him creep up to where they were sitting. `But I've got someone from one of the Sunday newspapers on the telephone for you. I told him that you were in a meeting but he said it was very important and quite urgent.'

`Did he say what it was about?' Mrs Caldicot asked him.

The assistant manager shook his head. `No, madam,' he said, `but he did ask me to make it clear to you that what he had to say to you would be to your advantage.' He smiled.

`All right,' said Mrs Caldicot, `Thank you.' She stood up. `Excuse me for a moment,' she said to Derek and Veronica. `Help yourself to tea,' she said, nodding towards the tray. `I'll be back in just a minute.'

***

`Is that Mrs Caldicot?' asked a gruff voice on the telephone. The voice had a faint Welsh lilt to it.

Mrs Caldicot confirmed that he was, indeed, speaking to Mrs Caldicot.

`My name is Jenkins,' said the gruff voice with the Welsh lilt. `I work for the *Sunday Journal*. I want to make you famous and give you lots of money.'

`I beg your pardon?' laughed Mrs Caldicot.

`Really!' said Jenkins. `I want to make you rich and famous.'

`Why on earth would you want to do that?'

`My editor saw you on the Mike Trickle Show yesterday evening and again on the breakfast programme this morning. He loved you. He wants us to run your life story in the paper.'

Mrs Caldicot laughed out loud.

`I'm serious,' said Jenkins. `What my editor wants he gets.'

'I don't think I want my life story in any paper,' protested Mrs Caldicot. 'I don't think I want to be famous.'

'Well you may not be able to have your wish,' said Jenkins. 'If you won't cooperate with us I know what my editor will do.'

'What?' asked Mrs Caldicot, slightly alarmed now. Although she was not a regular reader of the *Sunday Journal* she had seen it occasionally lining drawers and wrapped around chips. The newspaper had a reputation for publishing stories which the people involved didn't usually want printing.

'He'll tell me to put a couple of reporters onto your story and to dig out what we can,' said Jenkins. 'There are two advantages to you if you cooperate with us. First, you get to tell us what you want us to print. And second we give you money.'

It did sound convincing and Mrs Caldicot certainly did need the money. 'How much money?' she asked.

'We'll talk about that over lunch,' said Jenkins, very businesslike. 'I'll meet you at one o'clock in the restaurant at your hotel. I've booked a table in my name. O.K.?'

'I suppose so,' agreed Mrs Caldicot, rather bowled over by it all.

***

'What was all that about?' demanded Derek, when his mother returned from the telephone. He put down his tea cup.

'It was a man from the *Sunday Journal*,' explained Mrs Caldicot. 'They want to publish my life story.' She picked up the teapot and poured herself a cup of tea.

'Oh my God!' said Veronica. 'Oh my God! the *Sunday Journal*.' She looked around as though already expecting the strangers passing by to be staring at her.

'Wow!' said Jason, looking up and speaking. It had been so long since he had spoken that Mrs Caldicot did not recognise his voice. '*Sunday Journal*!' he said.

'Shut up, Jason!' snapped Veronica.

Jason shut up and went back to his magazine. Mrs Caldicot was impressed by his hearing acuity for throughout this short exchange Jason had continued to listen to the tinny noise emanating from his closely fitting headphones.

'I hope you said 'no', mother!' said Derek.

`I didn't,' said Mrs Caldicot, sipping at her tea. `I'm having lunch with a man called Mr Jenkins and I'm going to listen to what he has to say.'

`Tell her, Derek!' said Veronica firmly. `Tell her that unless she stops all this nonsense straight away...' She paused, searching in vain for a threat with which to complete the sentence.

`Tell me what?' said Mrs Caldicot.

`We won't have anything more to do with you!' said Veronica, defiantly. `We'll disown you. Tell her Derek.'

`You're being very selfish, mother,' whined Derek. `I've got a reputation to uphold. You're not making it easy for me.'

`I'm sorry if I'm an embarrassment to you,' said Mrs Caldicot, standing up. And then she walked briskly away.

CHAPTER EIGHTEEN

It was still not ten o'clock when Mrs Caldicot got back to her room. She had three hours before she was due to have lunch with Mr Jenkins from the *Sunday Journal*. Searching for something to read she idly picked up a red plastic folder containing menus and details of the facilities that the Mettleham Grand Hotel had to offer. When she saw that the hotel had its own swimming pool and Sports and Leisure Complex she decided to see whether Miss Nightingale, Mrs Peterborough and the others wanted to try it out. Support for this unplanned excursion into fitness training was unanimous and fifteen minutes later a slightly apprehensive Mrs Caldicot, whose only previous practical experience of sport had been thirty minutes on a council owned grass tennis court some fifty five years previously, led a straggly, and rather untidy looking procession down the stairs and into the hotel Sports and Leisure Complex.

The swimming pool and gym area were empty, as they usually were in mid-morning, except for two middle aged women. Both were hoping to lose unwanted lumps and wrinkles, accumulated in thirty years of dissolute and lazy living, in as many minutes. Massaged, soothed, pampered and oiled they were now recovering from their exhausting ordeal and relaxing on reclining chairs by the side of the pool. Their husbands were busy upstairs in a meeting room on the first floor. They were trying to persuade the owner of a local supermarket chain to hire their agency's advertising and promotional skills.

The manager of the Sports and Leisure Complex, a plump woman of uncertain years who wore a white nylon coat, a white plastic name badge carrying both her title and her name, too much make-up and so much hair spray that if she had for some inexplicable reason decided to carry a pitcher of water on her head the bottom of the pitcher would have rested a good six inches from her skull, and who had been given the job because she evoked a feeling of empathy among the customers, paled when she saw Mrs Caldicot's army advancing towards her. Never before had she seen so many liver spots in the Sports and Leisure Complex. Her three slender, teenage assistants, all fully trained beauty therapists (boasting nearly seven months practical experience between them), lined up alongside her and wondered, not for the first time, whether they would not have been better advised to do the college course in dental hygiene.

`Can I help you, madam?' the manageress asked Mrs Caldicot, with slightly forced civility, wondering for just the briefest of suspicious moments whether or not she was playing unwilling hostess to an errant coach party.

`We would like to take advantage of your facilities, Mrs Townsend,' smiled Mrs Caldicot, leaning forward ten degrees and reading the manageress's name badge.

`Are you all staying in the hotel, madam?'

Mrs Caldicot confirmed that they were, indeed, all bona fide residents and, as such, entitled to enjoy the wholesome and uplifting facilities of the Sports and Leisure Complex.

The manageress lowered her eyes and her voice and leant forwards a degree or two. `Are all your...er...party...physically fit enough, do you think?' she asked, rather nervously.

`Oh, I think so,' smiled Mrs Caldicot. She looked around and noticed with a shimmer of apprehension that Mr Hewitt had unfastened the cord around his dressing gown and was clearly preparing to dive into the pool. Her apprehension was inspired by the knowledge that Mr Hewitt was almost certainly not the owner of any suitable swimwear. Her fear was fully justified when, a brief moment later, the dressing gown fell to the floor and Mr Hewitt's bony frame was revealed, guarded against accusations of indecency by nothing more substantial than a pair of grey and slightly moth-eaten underpants, the elasticated waistband of which had long since passed through `slack', gone past `baggy' and ventured into territory which could only be described as `unsafe'. She glanced towards the two reclining wives and noticed with some relief that in both cases their vision was substantially impeded by the presence of slices of cucumber. Mr Hewitt, uncluttered by such unnecessary emotional baggage as embarrassment, leapt gaily into the water and disappeared. When he reappeared a few moments later, spluttering and spitting, he announced amidst great gasps for breath that he could not swim. His audience froze in horror; fear and uncertainty turning them all into statues.

`Only joking!' cried Mr Hewitt a heart stopping moment later, wiping the water away from his eyes and splashing about in a determined and surprisingly athletic way.

Inspired by the fun his friend was clearly having Mr Livingstone unfastened his dressing gown and then realised, just in time, that he was still wearing his pyjamas. He walked over to where Mrs Caldicot was standing and whispered to her. `I haven't got any trunks!' he said.

Mrs Caldicot turned to the manageress. `Do you have any swimwear for sale?'

`Oh, yes, madam!' said the manageress. `We have a boutique.' She made this pronouncement with a considerable amount of pride, as though it were an exceptional facility for a Sports and Leisure Complex to boast; much in the same way, thought Mrs Caldicot, that she might have announced that the complex was equipped with a neutron particle accelerator or a planetarium.

While Mr Hewitt happily splashed and spluttered his way from one end of the pool to the other, Mr Livingstone, Mrs Caldicot, Miss Nightingale, Mrs Peterborough and the rest of the exiles went off in search of the boutique. During the next ten minutes they emerged in turn from the changing room dressed in the latest and most colourful swimwear.

`Put it all on my bill,' murmured Mrs Caldicot to the boutique assistant, a pretty but rather moody and sour faced girl who had fallen out with her boyfriend the night before, with the comforting knowledge that since she didn't have enough money to pay the bill that she already owed the Mettleham Grand Hotel the extra debt she was accumulating was of little real significance. She could never before remember feeling quite so liberated as far as money was concerned. Mr Caldicot had always been extraordinarily strict about financial matters, and as a lifelong supporter of the Micawber principle had always forbidden Mrs Caldicot to spend anything she didn't have in her purse. He had believed that money was to be savoured rather than spent but Mrs Caldicot was slowly discovering that whatever people may say about money not buying happiness money can be used to buy things, experiences and time - all of which can lead directly to happiness.

Having dipped a timid toe in the swimming pool water and deemed it too chilly for her taste Mrs Caldicot, proudly encircled by a colourful creation in a figure hugging fabric which revealed every curve and fold of her figure, headed for the massage tables. Miss Nightingale and Mrs Peterborough followed her.

The hour which followed was almost certainly the most relaxing, most peaceful and most rewarding that Mrs Caldicot had ever enjoyed. She lay for what seemed an eternity on a comfortable couch while a pair of young hands gently kneaded and calmed her muscles. She bathed in oils of lavender and orange and she relaxed in the soothing warmth of the sauna.

She emerged onto the area around the pool feeling like a new, revitalised woman and she heard a strange noise coming from within herself as she watched Mr Hewitt and Mr Livingstone fill the jacuzzi with the foam from tiny bottles which they had smuggled down from their bathrooms. She couldn't remember ever hearing herself make the sound before and it took her a few moments to realise that it was a giggle.

She was giggling like a happy schoolgirl.

All around her the refugees from The Twilight Years Rest Home were resting, relaxing or enjoying themselves. Mrs Caldicot could never remember seeing them enjoy themselves so much. It gave her a warm feeling inside.

The magic of the moment was broken by what sounded like an argument developing. Mrs Caldicot turned around and saw that Mrs Townsend, the Sports and Leisure Complex manageress, had become embroiled in an inescapable and unwinnable argument with Mrs Peterborough.

`I don't think there's any need to take that tone,' said Mrs Townsend, who did not know enough about Mrs Peterborough to realise that the former Twilight Years Rest Home resident would have happily argued with a speak your weight machine.

`I don't think there's any need to take that tone,' mimicked Mrs Peterborough.

`Well!' said Mrs Townsend, putting her neatly manicured hands on her ample hips and throwing her head back.

`Well!' said Mrs Peterborough, equally indignantly, putting her own arthritic fingers on her bony hips.

`This is outrageous!' cried Mrs Townsend.

`This is outrageous!' said Mrs Peterborough.

`Isn't it a lovely day,' said Mrs Caldicot calmly, leaping in between the two of them and smiling at Mrs Peterborough.

`Isn't it a lovely day,' said Mrs Peterborough, smiling back at Mrs Caldicot.

`Why don't we find a couple of those nice chairs and sit down by the pool,' said Mrs Caldicot to Mrs Peterborough, heading off for a quiet spot at the far corner of the pool area.

`Find a couple of chairs and sit down by the pool,' repeated Mrs Peterborough, following her.

`Well!' said Mrs Townsend to no one. `I don't know, I'm sure.'

Mrs Caldicot turned her head and gave the manageress a big smile.

`Look at me!' called Miss Nightingale.

Mrs Caldicot turned her head and looked. Miss Nightingale was sitting on an exercise bicycle. Mrs Caldicot walked over to see her followed closely by Mrs Peterborough.

`That looks fun!' said Mrs Caldicot.

`It is,' agreed Miss Nightingale. She leant her head to one side. `Though it's a little bit disappointing.'

`Why's that?' asked Mrs Caldicot. Mrs Peterborough climbed onto a second bicycle.

`No bell,' said Miss Nightingale. `I used to have a bicycle. It had a very loud bell.'

`You can make bell noises yourself!' Mrs Caldicot pointed out.

`Can I?'

`Yes.'

With a broad smile Miss Nightingale rang an imaginary bell. `Ring, ring!' she cried. `Ring, ring!'

`Ring, ring!' said Mrs Peterborough happily.

Mrs Caldicot smiled at them both and found somewhere quiet to sit down.

Twenty minutes later the reception desk sent a porter to tell Mrs Caldicot that a gentleman was waiting for her in the dining room.

As she left she could hear Miss Nightingale and Mrs Peterborough.

`Ring, ring!'

`Ring, ring!'

CHAPTER NINETEEN

`You don't look a bit like your voice!' said Mrs Caldicot to Mr Jenkins.

`What should look like?' asked the newspaperman with a grin.

`Oh, I don't know,' said Mrs Caldicot. She thought for a moment. `You sounded, well, much more earnest on the telephone.'

Jenkins was tall and broad shouldered, slightly balding (though the hair that he did have was much longer than Mr Caldicot ever wore his hair) and had a luxuriant moustache and a permanent twinkle in his eye. He looked rather distinguished but he definitely did not look earnest. He was in his early sixties. He wore an expensive looking dark blue suit but the jacket was rumpled and creased because he hadn't bothered to take it off on the train. Mr Caldicot had always kept a wooden coat hanger in his briefcases so that he could hang his jacket up when he was travelling. Jenkins' white shirt looked expensive, it had a small monogram on the breast, but his red silk tie was carelessly knotted.

He was sitting on a stool at the bar when Mrs Caldicot came down from her room where she had changed her clothes, brushed her hair and put some lipstick on. She apologised for being late. He smiled and said it really didn't matter and asked her what she wanted to drink. When she asked him what he was drinking he told her it was straight gin. She asked the bartender to put a little vermouth into hers because she didn't want to get `squiffy'. Jenkins put his head back and laughed. She had never seen anyone laugh like that before.

`I've never heard anyone use that word!' he said. `Squiffy!' he repeated, as though he liked the sound of the word, and he laughed again.

`You don't have a notebook or a tape recorder,' she pointed out. `I thought you'd probably have both.'

Jenkins took a gulp out of his glass and glowered at her in a mock serious sort of way. `I don't actually write anything,' he told her. `I'm far too important for that.' He slid off his bar stool and she realised that he was even taller than she'd thought. `Shall we go through and eat?' He had a huge pile of newspapers with him which he picked up off the floor.

`Are those all today's papers?' asked Mrs Caldicot.

`Yes,' said Jenkins. `And I haven't finished reading them yet.'

`Are you really important?' she asked him, as they walked towards the dining room.

He looked down at her, started to say something and then changed his mind. `In my world,' he said and shrugged. He paused. `I meant what I said on the telephone,' he told her. `I can make you rich and famous.'

The head waiter met them at the door to the restaurant, recognised Mrs Caldicot and escorted them to their table.

`Why on earth would I want to be famous?' asked Mrs Caldicot.

`Some people like being famous for the sake of it,' said Jenkins. `They like strangers recognising them in the street. They like to get the best tables in restaurants. There's a certain cachet in being a celebrity which some people find attractive, even irresistible.'

`Someone asked me for my autograph this morning,' she said. `I found it rather embarrassing.' The waiter pulled back a chair and she sat down.

`You might get used to it,' said Jenkins, sitting down opposite her. `Even hooked on it.'

`I doubt it,' said Mrs Caldicot.

`What about the money? Are you interested in money?'

`At the moment I am,' admitted Mrs Caldicot. `I still don't quite know how it happened but I've got sixteen rooms in this place to pay for.' She accepted a menu from a white-coated waiter. `And if and when we leave here I don't have the faintest idea what I'm going to do with Miss Nightingale, Mrs Peterborough, Mr Livingstone and all the rest of them.'

`Those are the people who came with you from `The Twilight Zone Rest Home'?'

`Years,' corrected Mrs Caldicot, laughing.

`Years?'

`You said `The Twilight Zone Rest Home',' said Mrs Caldicot. `It's The Twilight Years Rest Home. And, yes, those are the people who came with me.'

`Are they happy here?'

`Yes, I think so. Though Miss Nightingale and Mrs Peterborough would like bells on their exercise bicycles.'

Jenkins laughed and pointed to the menu. `Shall we order?'

***

Forty minutes later Jenkins sat back, picked the rumpled napkin off his lap and tossed it onto the table. `I enjoyed that!' he said. He had eaten, with evident enjoyment, a huge bowl of soup, a mixed grill, and a large plateful of cheese and biscuits. Mrs Caldicot had eaten a prawn cocktail and a cheese salad but had obtained considerable pleasure from watching Mr Jenkins. Mr Caldicot had never really enjoyed his food.

`I don't think I've ever drunk so much wine!' said Mrs Caldicot, feeling not unpleasantly lightheaded. `Do you newspaper people always drink so much?'

Jenkins looked surprised. `We only had two bottles between us!'

`That's a lot!'

`There's evidence now to show that wine is good for your health,' said Jenkins. `Stops you getting heart attacks; that's what our doc says.'

`Your doc?'

`The chap who writes our medical column. He says that's why the French don't get heart disease.'

`Because they drink lots of wine?'

Jenkins nodded.

`Maybe it's because they all die of cirrhosis before they can get heart disease.'

Jenkins laughed. `I like our doctor's theory better.' He pushed his chair back an inch or two. `Shall we have coffee in the lounge?' A waiter, who had been hovering nearby, leapt forwards to attend to Mrs Caldicot's chair.

`That would be nice,' said Mrs Caldicot.

They walked slowly through the restaurant to the lounge. Jenkins took her arm to help steer her in between the tables and Mrs Caldicot, who felt more than a little `squiffy', was grateful.

`I enjoyed that very much,' she said, as they settled down into easy chairs. `Thank you.'

`You hardly ate anything!'

`I enjoyed watching you eat.'

`I like my food.'

`I could see that!' Mrs Caldicot blushed. `Oh, I'm sorry,' she apologised. `Was that rude?'

`Not at all!' laughed Jenkins.

`It's very nice eating in a smart restaurant,' said Mrs Caldicot. `I haven't done much of that you know.'

`You should do more,' said Jenkins, serious for a moment.

`I can't afford this sort of life,' said Mrs Caldicot, equally seriously.

`You could,' said Jenkins. He took a metal cigar tube out of his inside jacket pocket. `Do you mind if I smoke?'

Mrs Caldicot shook her head. She didn't like cigarettes but she quite enjoyed the smell of cigars. A waiter brought their coffee and Mrs Caldicot told him that she would pour. While Jenkins took his cigar out of its protective case, snipped the end off and lit it, she poured two cups of coffee, unwrapped the chocolate that was in her saucer and popped it into her mouth. Jenkins, his cigar alight, took the chocolate from his saucer and put it into hers. She mouthed a silent thank you.

`Eight million people saw you on the Mike Trickle show,' said Jenkins, leaning back in his chair and crossing his legs. `And another million and a half saw you on the breakfast programme.' He paused and puffed at his cigar. `You're big news.'

`My fifteen minutes of fame,' said Mrs Caldicot.

`Not necessarily,' Jenkins corrected her.

Mrs Caldicot sipped at her coffee, tried to resist the temptation to unwrap the other chocolate and waited.

`We want your life story. How did a perfectly ordinary woman...,' he looked at Mrs Caldicot and made an apologetic gesture. She dismissed the gesture with one of her own. `Perfectly ordinary you are not,' he said, correcting himself. `What sort of woman ends up leading a revolution in a nursing home, living in a four star hotel with heaven knows how many old people and humiliating two TV hosts?'

`Golly!' said Mrs Caldicot. `When you put it like that...'

`We'll pay you £10,000 for your story,' said Jenkins. `We'll run it over two, maybe three, weeks; we'll run what you tell us and we'll protect you from the rat pack.'

Mrs Caldicot felt faint. She had never envisaged her story being worth that sort of money. `What's a rat pack?' she asked, trying hard to stay in touch with reality.

'Other journalists,' explained Jenkins. 'When your story appears you'll be a major star. You'll have reporters from Germany, Japan and the States clamouring for your story. We can handle all that for you.'

'I don't know,' said Mrs Caldicot in a very faint voice which she hardly recognised as her own. 'It's a risky thing to do,' she thought. 'What if they make me out to be a terrible person? And do I really want to be recognised and talked about in the supermarket?' She looked at Jenkins but didn't say anything.

'I'm 71,' she thought to herself. 'I could have a quarter of my life left. Just because I've wasted the first three quarters doesn't mean that I've got to waste the rest being careful. £10,000 is a lot of money. And what have I got to lose?' She realised that she wanted to get her money's worth out of life and she decided to say 'yes'.

'Yes.' she said. 'All right. I'll do it.'

'It's a fair offer,' said Jenkins. 'I'll be honest with you, when I came here I was going to offer you £3,000.' He leant forward, 'You would have taken it, wouldn't you?'

At first Mrs Caldicot didn't know what to say. She had no idea how much money her story was worth to a newspaper. She hadn't really thought of it as being worth anything. In the end she was just honest. 'Probably,' she admitted. 'Yes, I suppose so.'

'I'll tell the editor that you pushed me up to ten,' shrugged Jenkins. 'Easy. It's not my money.'

'But why?' asked Mrs Caldicot.

'I like you,' grinned Jenkins. 'And I'm not as gruff as my voice!' He puffed at his cigar. 'Have we got a deal?'

'Yes,' said Mrs Caldicot, in a very quiet voice. Jenkins had to lean across to hear her. 'Yes!' she said. 'Thank you.'

'Right!' said Jenkins. 'Let's celebrate with some bubbly.' He waved an arm for the waiter.

Mrs Caldicot, already feeling more than 'squiffy' thought she probably needed to have more food in her stomach if she was going to drink any more alcohol and so she picked up the second chocolate, unwrapped it and popped it into her mouth.

CHAPTER TWENTY

Mrs Caldicot woke up at six o'clock on Sunday morning, used the tea making facilities in her room and waited for the porter to push her copy of the *Sunday Journal* underneath the door.

When the newspaper finally arrived it came through so speedily, flicked skilfully on its way by the porter's agile fingers, that it startled her. She stared at it for several moments without moving. She hardly dared to pick it up and she could feel her heart beating uncomfortably rapidly. She had never been frightened by a newspaper before.

The reporter from the *Sunday Journal* had arrived the day after Mrs Caldicot had lunch with Jenkins and had stayed for two days. To her surprise the reporter had been a woman; or rather a girl. Everything about the *Sunday Journal* seemed to surprise her. She had expected a middle aged man in a grubby suit. But she got a svelte young woman dressed in a simple Chanel dress who had turned the head of every businessman in the hotel bar. She had expected a rather beery, leery reporter with a love of football and scandal and a penchant for cheap thrillers and dirty movies. But she got a sophisticated graduate with a degree in French Literature and a fondness for seventeenth century poetry. She had expected questions that would make her feel uncomfortable and embarrassed. She had been ready to say 'No, stop, enough, go away!' But the girl reporter talked to her like a friend and asked her nothing she did not talk about easily and comfortably.

Cautiously, almost reluctantly, Mrs Caldicot stood up, moved forwards, bent down and picked up the newspaper. She took it back to her chair and sat down with it on her lap. Still she didn't look at it.

When she did finally look down she saw her face staring out at her from a panel on the right hand side of the front page. It was a lovely photograph. Above the photograph her name was printed in large bold letters. Below it the paper promised all. The inside story. The truth. Mrs Caldicot stared at it and felt her mouth go dry. In that moment she wished she had not had anything to do with the *Sunday Journal*. She wished she had never cut the chrysanthemums; never refused to eat Mr Fuller-Hawksmoor's cabbage; never agreed to go on television.

But she had done all those things. It was too late now to wish that she had not.

With trembling fingers she opened the paper, wondering whether the guilty vicar and the scoutmaster's wife, the naughty comedian with a penchant for young boys, the blushing TV starlet with a history she would have liked to forget, the compromised politician and the stripping housewife from Rochdale were at this moment sitting in their kitchens sharing her anxiety. How many of them, she wondered, were ensconced in lonely hotel rooms. Or was she the only one who had to face this ordeal alone. She felt an affinity for them all; a forgiveness and an affection for every one of them. Perhaps, she thought, there should be an organisation for people who have had their private, and most personal details discussed in the Sunday newspapers. A telephone number to ring for support. Meetings to attend. Social workers to give endless advice.

But would she be entitled to support and comfort and advice? She was there willingly. She had exposed herself to public scrutiny for money. She doubted if the politician or the television actress accused of infidelity had been paid for their downfall. The vicar wouldn't have a cheque for £10,000 to settle his nerves, help soothe away the inconvenience and pay for his ruined life.

Eventually she reached her story. They had spread it over a double page with a promise of more to come. The girl reporter's name was there but in much smaller letters than her own. She remembered the money they had agreed to pay her. It seemed a lot of money for so little. And yet was it so little? She looked at the photographs. A picture of her alone. A picture of her with Kitty. There was a photograph of the outside of The Twilight Years Rest Home with an angry looking Mr Fuller-Hawksmoor bearing down on the photographer with a big stick. She even recognised the stick. It usually stood in the hall-stand. Abandoned, no doubt, by some long lost resident. She read the captions and then read the little snippets that the sub editor had picked out to highlight in boxes. It was her life, laid bare for everyone to see. She felt that it was worse, far worse, than being seen naked in public. She started to read the story from the end and as she did so Kitty, who had been asleep on the bed, walked over to her and curled up on her lap.

There was nothing in there that wasn't true; nothing that she was ashamed of: but it felt strange to read about her private moments, private thoughts and private apprehensions in such a public place. She felt exposed and vulnerable.

The telephone rang.

The sudden, harsh, noise startled her. Kitty raised her head.

She put down the newspaper and picked up the receiver.

`Hello. What do you think?' It was Jenkins.

`I'm terrified,' said Mrs Caldicot.

`I thought you would be.' He sounded kinder than he usually did on the telephone.

`It makes me feel naked.'

`I know. Have you read it?'

`Not properly. I've looked at it.'

`Any complaints?'

She paused. `Not about what it says. It seems fair.' She caught sight of the digital clock next to the telephone. It was still not seven o'clock. A thought occurred to her. `How did you know I would be awake? How did you know I would have seen the paper?'

Jenkins laughed.

`I suppose everyone's the same,' said Mrs Caldicot.

`In London you can buy the Sunday papers at the railway stations on a Saturday evening,' said Jenkins. `Some people come down especially to buy them.'

`I didn't know that.'

`I know. I thought of telling you. But decided you'd probably rather be where you are when you first saw the paper.'

`I don't know.'

`Don't know what?'

`Whether I would rather have seen it here or been in London.'

`Have you had breakfast yet?'

`No. Oh no. I won't dare go down. I'll have to get them to send something up. I don't think I can eat anyway.'

`Go down,' said Jenkins firmly. `Have your breakfast in the restaurant.'

`But everyone will be staring at me!'

`They won't. I know we go on about our circulation but not everyone reads the *Sunday Journal*. And even the people who do read it won't necessarily recognise you.'

Mrs Caldicot said nothing.

'Really,' said Jenkins. 'One in five adults in the country sees our paper. Some of those only read the sport pages. Some just look for the juicy, sexy scandals. One in five will read the story about you in any detail. And less than one in ten of those will remember your name an hour after they've read the story.'

'Really?'

'The number who will actually recognise you from your photograph is minuscule!'

'I suppose I could change my hair a bit,' said Mrs Caldicot, who still didn't really believe this.

'Just don't wear anything you're wearing in any of the photos,' advised Jenkins.

'Will this feeling go away?'

'How do you feel?'

'As if I've been violated. Much worse than having been on television.'

'Do you wish you hadn't done it?'

'Yes. At the moment.'

'What are you going to do today?'

'I don't know.'

'Would you come out with me for some lunch?'

Mrs Caldicot was taken aback. She didn't know what to say and so didn't say anything.

'Are you still there?'

'Yes,' she said. 'Yes. I'd like that. But why? I mean, haven't you got a family to be with?'

'I don't want you to be alone,' said Jenkins. 'Professional responsibility. And I'd prefer to have lunch with you.'

'What about your wife? Won't she mind?'

'I doubt it. She lives in Cornwall with a potter.'

'Oh. I'm sorry.'

'Don't be. It's been over a long time.' Jenkins paused. 'Go and have some breakfast. I'll pick you up about eleven thirty and we'll drive out into the country somewhere.'

'All right!' she heard herself say. 'Thank you.' She put the telephone down.

It rang again. It was the receptionist with her early morning call.

'You asked for an early morning call at seven,' said the

anonymous but kindly sounding voice. `I'm sorry it's a few minutes late but I couldn't get through. Your phone was busy.'

`I was talking to someone.'

`It's five minutes past seven now,' said the receptionist.

`Thank you.' said Mrs Caldicot. `What time does breakfast start.'

`Half past seven on Sundays.'

`Thank you,' said Mrs Caldicot. She put the telephone down, gently moved Kitty back onto the bed, went into the bathroom, bathed, put on her make-up, found a beige jumper and tweed skirt that she hadn't been photographed in and got dressed. By the time she'd done all that it was twenty five minutes past seven. She left her room and went down to breakfast. It was, she thought, probably one of the bravest things she'd ever done. It was also, she knew, one of the most sensible. If she had stayed hidden in her room she would have probably never left it.

CHAPTER TWENTY ONE

At breakfast no one had as much as looked in her direction. She knew this for a fact because she had been waiting for people to stare at her, to nudge one another and to whisper about her.

But no one did. She ate her croissants and her muesli and she drank two cups of coffee quite uninterrupted and unthreatened by her notoriety.

When she went back up to her room three-quarters of an hour later she was feeling much happier. That was when Derek telephoned.

`What on earth are you trying to do?' he spluttered. He then said something completely incoherent. He sounded as if he was about to burst a blood vessel.

`Slow down, dear,' said Mrs Caldicot, calmly. `What's the matter?'

`You know damned well what the matter is!' exploded Derek. `This rubbish in the *Sunday Journal*!'

`Why do you think it's rubbish?' asked Mrs Caldicot.

`It's in the *Sunday Journal*!' said Derek. `Everything in the *Sunday Journal* is rubbish!'

`Don't be silly, dear,' said Mrs Caldicot. `That's just prejudice. Have you read it?'

`Of course I've read it!' said Derek. `What was all that nonsense about my father?'

`Only the truth, dear,' said Mrs Caldicot quietly.

`Who do you think is interested in all that stuff?' demanded Derek.

`I don't know,' confessed Mrs Caldicot honestly.

`You have your picture taken and tell your life story as if you're a film star!' complained Derek. `It's not as if you're a woman of any significance!'

`That's what the people at the *Sunday Journal* said,' replied Mrs Caldicot coldly. `It took me quite a time to persuade them to print it. They wanted to do a story about someone interesting.'

`I didn't mean that,' said Derek, almost apologetically. `But you know what I mean.'

`I know what you mean,' said Mrs Caldicot, unmollified. `I'm not of any significance.'

`Oh stop being so selfish, mother!' said Derek. `Why don't you think of someone else for a change?'

`You, perhaps?'

`Yes! How do you think all this makes me look? I'm trying to build up a reputation as a serious businessman and you're making me look silly.'

`I'm sorry you feel that way,' said Mrs Caldicot. `I didn't think the story made either of us look silly at all.'

`Oh there's no point in trying to talk to you!' said Derek angrily. `I've got to go. I've got better things to do than talk nonsense with you.'

`What is it, dear? Have you got to wash the car or are you playing golf?'

Mrs Caldicot winced as Derek slammed the telephone down. Then she realised that she felt good, better than she'd felt all morning. If she'd ever learned how to whistle she would have whistled. She went round to check on Miss Nightingale, Mrs Peterborough and the others before Jenkins turned up to take her out to lunch.

***

`You're looking brighter than you sounded this morning!' said Jenkins. He was still wearing his expensive but slightly rumpled suit. He smelt faintly of aftershave; a modest indication that this was at least partly a social occasion.

`I feel brighter!' said Mrs Caldicot. She had abandoned the tweed skirt and beige jumper and was wearing a favourite pale green dress which had a dozen buttons down the back. She'd worn it for some of the photographs that had appeared in the *Sunday Journal*.

`What happened this morning?' asked Jenkins as they walked through the hotel reception area and out to the car park. He recognised the dress but did not say so.

`Nothing!' said Mrs Caldicot. She paused. `Well, that's not true. My son rang. But apart from that you don't seem to have any readers around here.'

`What did your son say?' asked Jenkins. `Did he object?'

`Oh, he objected all right!' said Mrs Caldicot. `But I've decided that I don't care.'

`Good for you!' said Jenkins.

There was a sudden noise, sounding like a good many knuckles being rapped against window panes. Mrs Caldicot and Jenkins both turned. Lined up against the glass walls of the swimming pool area Mrs Caldicot could see Mrs Peterborough, Miss Nightingale and the rest of her gang of refugees. They were all grinning, waving furiously and rapping their knuckles against the glass. They were wearing their new swim suits.

`Good heavens! Said Jenkins. `Who on earth are they?'

`My friends from The Twilight Years Rest Home,' explained Mrs Caldicot.

Jenkins looked embarrassed. `Oh, yes. Sorry! What are they up to?'

`They discovered the Sport and Leisure Complex,' explained Mrs Caldicot. `Remember? I told you that Miss Nightingale and Mrs Peterborough wanted bells for the exercise bicycles. I think they're planning to spend the day there.' She looked back at the grinning faces and waved. `It's funny,' she said, `when you're young you know you're getting older because the policemen and the supermarket managers and then the doctors look younger and younger, but you know you're really old when the old people look young.'

Jenkins looked at her and smiled and then stopped alongside a large but dirty motor car. It had been blue when it had left the showroom but, spattered with mud and oil and dirt had become a road weary grey. `Close your eyes to the mess,' he said. `I keep meaning to get it cleaned...' his voice trailed off apologetically. He opened his door and turned the key. Mrs Caldicot waited for him to reach across and open the passenger door. The inside of the car was a mess too; there was a pile of newspapers strewn across the back seat and the floor was covered with sweet papers and cigar ash, cigar packets and spent matches.

`It's open,' he told her. He reached over to the back seat and tried to tidy up the newspapers. `I'm sorry,' he said again. `I should have cleaned all this stuff up.'

`It's all right,' said Mrs Caldicot. `I quite like it.' Mr Caldicot had been very particular about the inside of his car. He didn't allow smoking and he always had one of those little perfumed cards hanging from the driving mirror. Mrs Caldicot had always thought they made the Vauxhall smell of lavatories.

`I've booked a table at a pub I know,' said Jenkins. `It's by the river, and if the weather holds we can eat outside. It's very pretty. I think you'll like it.' He put the car into gear and shot out of the Mettleham Grand Hotel car park as though making a getaway from a bank robbery. Mrs Caldicot, pressed against the back of her seat, struggled to fasten her safety belt. `It's very kind of you to look after me like this,' she said trying to relax as Jenkins swung the big car out onto the road between a small Ford and a van.

`All part of the service,' smiled Jenkins but somehow Mrs Caldicot knew it wasn't. He drove at a speed which both terrified and thrilled Mrs Caldicot, and although he took chances and seemed oblivious to the existence and rights of other road users he drove with an easy, nonchalant skill. He pointed out strange landmarks. Not dull things like buildings of minor architectural interest or the sites of Roman forts but a house where there had been a murder, a church where the vicar had been caught misbehaving with the choir mistress and a lonely field where a body had been found. He was an inexhaustible fund of wonderful trivia. Mrs Caldicot didn't believe half of it but that didn't matter in the slightest. Jenkins was funny, he made her laugh. She realised yet again, with an aching sadness, that Mr Caldicot had never, ever made her laugh.

God was smiling on them. As they pulled into the tiny car park next to the riverside pub the sun shone brightly. They sat at a white metal table, with the clear river running just a few feet away from them and ordered trout cooked with almonds, locally grown vegetables and a bottle of cool, dry white wine. Mrs Caldicot could not help remembering that Mr Caldicot had always refused to order wine in restaurants. He said they charged too much for it. They ate strawberries in meringue nests drenched in thick cream, drank double brandies and sipped dark, thick, bitter coffee.

Afterwards they walked in dappled shade by the river. Jenkins took his jacket off and carried it over his shoulder with his finger hooked into the loop at the back. They sat on mossy covered rocks underneath a huge oak tree, threw twigs into the water and watched them float down river. They watched, in silent amazement, as a kingfisher dived into the water and came up with a small fish in its beak. And then they walked slowly back along the bank.

Jenkins talked to her about his work; about the bizarre life he lived, close enough to power to smell it but just far enough away to remain uncorrupted by it; about the people he had met; about the stories he had worked on and the books he wanted to write when he retired from newspapers and bought a cottage in the country.

And he listened to her too. He asked her things and seemed genuinely interested in the answers. For the first time in years Mrs Caldicot felt important as a person rather than a cook, a laundress and a housekeeper. Slowly she realised what she had missed in her loveless and friendless marriage; she had shared her life with a man, but the sharing had been shallow and superficial. It hadn't been the way it could have been, should have been. She had, she realised, missed having someone to share things with; missed having someone to whom she could say, `Hey, you'll never guess what happened to me today!'; missed having someone she could laugh with; missed having someone she could wait for to tell about a funny story she'd seen in the paper or heard about on the radio; missed having someone with whom she could share the good, the bad and the trivial in her life. She realised that if she had shared her life with someone like Jenkins she would have doubled the amount of joy she felt and halved the amount of despair she had had to endure.

Jenkins drove her back to her hotel in the dusk and when they said goodbye he reached out and held her hand for a brief moment. He moved forwards and for an instant she thought he was going to kiss her cheek but he didn't. `Goodnight,' he said softly. `It hasn't been too bad a day, after all, has it?'

`No,' she said, smiling. `It hasn't been too bad at all.'

And as she watched him drive away she realised that she wouldn't have minded if he had kissed her goodnight.

Miss Nightingale and Mrs Peterborough were waiting for her in the reception area.

`We had a wonderful time!' said Miss Nightingale, her eyes full of excitement.

`We had a wonderful time!' agreed Mrs Peterborough.

`It was a pity you couldn't stay here,' said Miss Nightingale, speaking as rapidly as she could. `We all had a massage and we spent four hours in the jacuzzi! I was all wrinkly when I got out.'

`I was all wrinkly when I got out!' said Mrs Peterborough.
`It was so sad that you had to go out!' said Miss Nightingale.
`It was so sad that you had to go out!' said Mrs Peterborough.
`I know,' said Mrs Caldicot. `It was a shame, wasn't it?'
But that was a lie.

CHAPTER TWENTY TWO

Mrs Caldicot's room at the Mettleham Grand Hotel seemed quite
large when there was only her in it but with all the refugees from
The Twilight Years Rest Home crowded in with her the room was as
crammed as an excursion train on a bank holiday.

`We can't stay here much longer,' said Mrs Caldicot when she
finally managed to get them to stop talking.

There was a communal, almost orchestrated sigh of sadness.

`It's very expensive,' said Mrs Caldicot. `The TV company paid
for our first night but since then the bills have been mounting. And
the money I got from the *Sunday Journal* won't last forever.' She
paused. `We've got to find somewhere else,' she concluded.

`We don't expect you to pay our bills!' said Mr Livingstone.

`Certainly not!' protested Mr Hewitt, and although you could not
describe him as indignant there was certainly a touch of hurt in his
voice.

`Certainly not!' agreed Mrs Peterborough.

`We can all pay our own bills,' said Mr Livingstone.

`We've done our sums,' said Mr Hewitt. `And there's no problem.
It cost us more to stay at The Twilight Years Rest Home than it costs
us to stay here.'

`We're just going to arrange for our banks to pay the hotel instead
of Mr Fuller-Hawksmoor,' said Mr Livingstone.

`Oh!' said Mrs Caldicot, quite taken aback. She hadn't expected
any of this. She had never really thought about the fact that the other
residents of The Twilight Years Rest Home had been paying fairly
hefty amounts of money to stay there. She found herself wondering
why they had all allowed themselves to be pushed around and
bullied by Mr Fuller-Hawksmoor when they had been paying the
bills and had a right to expect good service. She wondered how
many thousands of old people up and down the country were
similarly ill treated.

`But we'll move if you want us to,' said Mrs Torridge agreeably.
Mrs Torridge was, at 63 years of age, probably one of the youngest
of the group. She had been put into the Twilight Years Rest Home

by her daughter and son-in-law who had immediately sold her home, pocketed the money and run off to New Zealand. Unbeknown to them, however, she had anticipated this example of filial disloyalty and stashed a more than adequate sum in gilt edged bonds. Mrs Torridge was joyfully overweight and indomitably cheerful. She paused. `As long as there's a jacuzzi!' she laughed. Mrs Caldicot could see the fluorescent orange of Mrs Torridge's new bathing suit spilling out from the canvas holdall beside her chair. There was, thought Mrs Caldicot, probably enough material in the bathing costume to make a tent for the average family of four. Mrs Caldicot had never seen anything quite as remarkable as the sight of Mrs Torridge in a bathing suit; it was a larger than life vision which was at once both intimidating and cheering.

`I had wondered about looking for somewhere for us to rent,' said Mrs Caldicot, pushing the vision of Mrs Torridge to one side. `A large house maybe?' She paused and looked around. Everyone was trying to look interested but they could not hide their disappointment.

`We don't have to move,' she added. `Especially if there isn't a problem over the money.' She looked around and waited for someone else to say something. `But if we found somewhere of our own we could look after Miss Kershaw, Mr Oppenshaw, Mrs Entwhistle and the others.' These were the patients who had been too ill to move when Mrs Caldicot and the others had walked out of The Twilight Years Rest Home. `And don't forget,' she warned, `if any of us gets ill the Mettleham Grand Hotel will probably tell us to leave. If we had our own place we wouldn't have to worry about anything like that.'

There was a long silence.

`I think Mrs Caldicot is right,' said Mr Hewitt.

`She's right,' agreed Mr Livingstone.

`She's right!' said Mrs Peterborough.

`Could we find somewhere with a jacuzzi, do you think?' asked Mrs Torridge, speaking in a tiny little girl voice.

`Could we find somewhere with a jacuzzi?' asked Mrs Peterborough.

`I'm sure we could have one installed,' said Mrs Caldicot. `Even if we can't find a place that has got one already.' She paused. `And we could maybe find somewhere with a garden so that Mr Hewitt could show us how to grow our own vegetables!'

`That would be wonderful!' said Mr Hewitt, who had spent months unsuccessfully trying to persuade Mr Fuller-Hawksmoor to allow him to dig up a small area of lawn for the growing of decent vegetables.

Mrs Caldicot turned towards Mr Livingstone. `And if we had our own place you would be able to entertain us with musical evenings!'

Mr Livingstone beamed.

`I think we should leave it all up to Mrs Caldicot,' said Mrs Torridge. `I'm happy to go where she goes.'

`I agree!' said Mr Hewitt.

`I agree!' cried Mrs Peterborough, excitedly and noisily.

This sealed it. There were enthusiastic mumblings of affirmation from the others and it was agreed that while Mrs Caldicot planned their future the rest of them would go down to the Sports and Leisure Complex and enjoy themselves.

***

The moment they had gone Mrs Caldicot picked up the telephone and dialled Derek's number.

Derek was out and the receptionist put Mrs Caldicot through to a girl called Ingrid.

`I'm looking for a house,' Mrs Caldicot explained to Ingrid. `It must be quite large. An old hotel would be perfect.' She explained that she wanted somewhere with a large number of bedrooms, a little land of its own and several large reception rooms.

`Do you want to buy or rent, madam?' asked Ingrid.

`I had thought of renting,' said Mrs Caldicot. `But I suppose we could buy somewhere if the right place came up.' There was a pause while Ingrid wrote this down. Mrs Caldicot thought that Ingrid was probably the sort of person who would lick her pencil tip and then stick her tongue out of the corner of her mouth while she wrote.

`Do you have anywhere to sell, madam?' asked Ingrid eventually.

`No,' said Mrs Caldicot. `We're living in a hotel at the moment.'

`What's the name, madam?' asked Ingrid.

`My name?'

`Yes, please, madam.'

Mrs Caldicot told her.

`Would you spell that please, madam?' asked Ingrid.

Mrs Caldicot spelt her name.

`Thank you,' said Ingrid. `I'll pass the information on to Mr Caldicot when he returns from his meeting.'

`How do you spell that?' asked Mrs Caldicot, mischievously.

Ingrid spelt out Mr Caldicot's name without comprehension, irony or curiosity.

`Thank you,' said Mrs Caldicot.

`I'm sure he'll be in touch with you quite quickly,' said Ingrid, her voice laden with artificial sincerity and warmth.

`Thank you,' said Mrs Caldicot. She felt quite certain that Ingrid was a very attractive young woman.

***

Mrs Caldicot put her swimming costume and dressing gown on, picked up a towel and went downstairs to the Sports and Leisure Complex.

Miss Nightingale and Mrs Peterborough were sitting on the two exercise bicycles, ringing brand new shiny bells and happily waving to everyone who passed by. Mrs Torridge was taking up half the jacuzzi and Mr Hewitt and Mr Livingstone were splashing about in the swimming pool. Mrs Caldicot wandered over to the exercise bicycles.

`Where did you get those from?' she asked Miss Nightingale, nodding towards the bells.

`They were here when we arrived,' replied Miss Nightingale happily.

`Hello, Mrs Cardew!' smiled the manageress, her capped and polished teeth sparkling in the powerful artificial light of the pool area. `The bells were a gift from the *Sunday Journal*, she explained. She took a small gift card out of her white nylon overall and handed it to Mrs Caldicot. `From the *Sunday Journal*', it read. `With best wishes'.

Mrs Caldicot smiled at her and handed the card back. She turned as someone tapped her on the shoulder.

`You're on the television!' said a portly, middle aged woman in a mauve dressing gown. Her hair was wet and she was carrying a rolled up copy of *Vogue* magazine under her arm. It was an accusation rather than a statement and it certainly wasn't a question. A weedy, timid looking man stood behind her. He had no hair of any significance and carried a folded newspaper and a paperback book in his right hand.

Mrs Caldicot admitted, with some reluctance, that she had, indeed, been on the television.

`You're Jessica Richardson, aren't you!' said the woman, decisively.

`No,' said Mrs Caldicot. `I'm afraid I'm not.' She vaguely recognised the name and rather thought that it belonged to an actress who appeared in a soap opera.

`Oh yes you are!' insisted the woman with a conspiratorial wink. She turned round and spoke to her husband. `It's her!' she whispered.

`It's not,' said Mrs Caldicot. But this denial was simply ignored.

`Tell me,' said the woman leaning closer. She smelt strongly of talcum powder. `Tell me, what's Albert Peters really like?'

`I'm afraid I don't know,' said Mrs Caldicot.

`Oh go on with you!' said the woman with another wink. `I know who you are. I've seen you on the television.' She wasn't very good at winking and when she did it both her eyes closed. `He's lovely, isn't he? Do you get on, you know, in real life?'

`Yes,' said Mrs Caldicot, rather wearily, answering the sequence of questions with a single word.

`Can I have your autograph?' asked the woman. She took the magazine from under her arm and thrust it towards Mrs Caldicot.

`I'm afraid I haven't got a pen.'

`Norman. A pen.' said the woman. Her voice changed dramatically when she spoke to her husband. She talked to him as a child would speak to a naughty doll. The weedy looking man produced a ball point pen from his dressing gown pocket, stepped forward and offered it to the woman. The woman took it and handed the pen and the magazine to Mrs Caldicot.

`What would you like me to put?' asked Mrs Caldicot.

`From Jessica Richardson to Emily Turner,' said the woman. `You can add `with lots of love' if you like.'

Mrs Caldicot wrote the prescribed phrase and added the love. Then she handed the pen and the magazine back to the woman.

The woman looked at the inscription carefully and nodded knowingly. `There you are,' she said to Mrs Caldicot. `I told you that you were Jessica Richardson.' She held the pen out and her husband took it from her.

`You did,' agreed Mrs Caldicot.

The woman disappeared, her husband trailing along behind her like an obedient puppy. Mrs Caldicot slipped out of her dressing gown and lowered herself into the jacuzzi. Every time Miss Nightingale and Mrs Peterborough rang the bells on their exercise bicycles it reminded her of Jenkins. The bubbles tickled and refreshed her skin and she lay back, closed her eyes and thought with fondness of their walk together along the river bank.

CHAPTER TWENTY THREE

`What on earth is going on, mother?' asked Derek Caldicot. He sounded weary.

`I want to rent or buy somewhere big enough for us all to live in,' replied Mrs Caldicot, sitting on her bed. She had been about to get changed when the telephone had rung. She was going out to dinner with Jenkins. `I thought you'd be offended if I went to another estate agent.'

Derek let out air as though he was deflating.

`I'll go to another estate agent if you prefer,' offered Mrs Caldicot, brightly. She kicked off her shoes and examined a ladder in her tights.

Derek sighed. `Why can't you be like everyone else's mother?' he asked her.

`I never said that to you,' said Mrs Caldicot, offended.

`What? What are you on about now?'

`When you were little,' explained Mrs Caldicot. `I never said `why aren't you like the other children' to you.'

`I don't remember,' said Derek. He thought about this for a moment. `Anyway, I was never unlike the other children,' he said, rather defensively.

`Oh yes you were,' said Mrs Caldicot. `You were so worried about being different that you weren't like anyone else I ever knew.' She smiled to herself at the memory of Derek in short grey trousers bursting into tears because he couldn't decide whether he wanted to wear short or long grey socks. In the end, in a spirit of compromise that she had to admire, he had settled for long grey socks which he had pushed down around his ankles.

`We're not talking about me,' said Derek, defensively. `It isn't me who wants to buy a house big enough to share with a hundred incontinent old people.'

`Don't exaggerate,' said Mrs Caldicot, sharply. `There aren't any more than twenty or so altogether and none of them is incontinent.' She paused. `Well, very few of them anyway and those who are incontinent are only a little bit incontinent.'

`If you don't want to live in a rest home then what's wrong with a nice granny flat?' asked Derek.

`It's too late for that now,' said Mrs Caldicot. `I've got responsibilities.' She also realised that she found her responsibilities exciting and rewarding. And the risks which she knew were associated with the responsibilities didn't worry her anywhere near as much as they would have done a month or two earlier. She realised that excitement and risk go together like rain and rivers, and that you can't have one without the other.

`There's a wonderful new development on the Portland Road,' said Derek. `I can get you a one bedroom flatlet at a very competitive price. Kitchenette with refrigerator, microwave oven and the very latest type of waste disposal unit. You can put tin cans down it and they'll come out shredded. Small bathroom. Telephone point in the living room and the bedroom. Wonderful views.'

`I don't want a one bedroom flatlet,' said Mrs Caldicot, bluntly.

`You can see the municipal park from one of the living room windows,' said Derek. `You can see the ornamental flower clock in the summer. Well, the top left hand bit of it anyway.'

`I don't want a one bedroom flatlet,' repeated Mrs Caldicot. `Not even one which has a view of the municipal park.'

`How can anyone be only a little bit incontinent?' asked Derek suddenly. `They're either incontinent or they aren't incontinent.'

`People can be a bit drunk, can't they? Or a bit forgetful?'

`You don't seem to understand,' said Derek. `If you rent or buy somewhere large you'll be taking on all sorts of responsibilities.'

`I don't mind,' said Mrs Caldicot, who really didn't mind. `I can't let the others down now.'

`But you hardly know them, mother!' cried Derek. `You've only just met these people.'

`I like them,' she replied. `And they trust me.' No one had ever really trusted her before. People had relied on her to do things but they had never trusted her. Mr Caldicot had relied on her to provide him with clean shirts and hot meals but he had never trusted her to make any decisions. And life with him had been so boring. He always wore plain white shirts and his meals had to rotate according to a strict and pre-arranged pattern. One Christmas she bought him a shirt with a thin blue stripe in it. He never wore it.

`That's all very well but where are you going to find the money from?' demanded Derek.

'We're all going to pay our share,' replied Mrs Caldicot. 'Money isn't going to be a problem.'

'It's bound to be risky. If you sign anything you'll be taking a chance.'

'What's the point of life if you don't take chances?' asked Mrs Caldicot.

'What on earth do you mean by that?' asked Derek. 'Why do you want to take chances at your age?'

'Perhaps because I haven't taken enough chances at any other age,' said Mrs Caldicot. 'Perhaps because at my age it doesn't really matter what chances I take. What have I got to lose?'

Derek sighed in defeat. 'I'll ask our commercial department to see what they can find. A man called Gerald will phone you.' There was a pause. 'I wash my hands of this, mother,' he said and put the phone down. Mrs Caldicot knew he was upset because he didn't even say 'goodbye'.

***

That evening Jenkins took Mrs Caldicot to the ballet to watch a performance of Swan Lake. Afterwards he took her to an Indian restaurant. She had never been to a ballet before nor had she ever eaten in an Indian restaurant.

'Don't you like it? asked Jenkins.

Mrs Caldicot, who had been staring into space without seeing anything, focused her attention on her dinner partner. He seemed blurred and she was suddenly aware that she had tears in her eyes.

'The food,' he explained. He nodded to her plate, virtually untouched.

'It's very good,' she assured him.

'Are you all right?' he asked, concerned. He reached across the table and touched the back of her left hand lightly with the tips of his own right hand.

Mrs Caldicot turned her hand over, grasped his fingers and squeezed them gently. 'I'm fine,' she whispered. She looked at him for a long, long moment. 'I just don't remember ever being quite so happy,' she explained. When she'd spoken she felt embarrassed, though she did not really know why.

`Penny for them,' said Jenkins.

Mrs Caldicot didn't answer straight away.

`Penny for your thoughts,' Jenkins explained unnecessarily.

For a moment Mrs Caldicot still didn't answer. `It's been a beautiful evening,' she said, her voice hoarse with emotion. `I've never done anything like this before,' she added. She tried to stop the tears because she didn't want to cry.

`You must have been to the theatre even if you haven't seen a ballet!'

Mrs Caldicot shook her head. `My husband and I didn't do things like that,' she said. Her voice felt stronger.

`But when you were younger? When you were courting?'

`We went to the cinema a few times.' She shrugged. `Westerns mainly...,' She looked at him and smiled. `I'm not complaining,' she said. `My husband never treated me badly.' He hadn't. He had never hit her. Never publicly criticised her.

`It gives me a lot of pleasure to be with you,' said Jenkins softly. She suddenly realised that she was still holding his hand. Slowly, she relaxed her grip. But his fingers did not move away from hers.

`Don't let your meal go cold,' said Mrs Caldicot.

They both ate. Mrs Caldicot was glad he hadn't said anything else. She enjoyed their silences together. She wasn't sure enough of herself to be able to share her feelings with him yet.

Afterwards, he drove her home. It had been raining and the streets were glistening. The reflections of the street lights sparkled on the wet pavements and she thought how romantic everywhere looked. Even buildings which in the brightness of daylight seemed drab and dull seemed strangely exciting in the darkness of the night. She did not mention any of this to him because she was slightly embarrassed at having such silly and romantic thoughts.

When they said goodnight he kissed her on both cheeks as she'd seen French people do on television and he held both her hands in his and squeezed them lightly.

Long after she'd climbed into bed she lay awake going over every moment of the evening in her mind. At twenty past two in the morning she realised that the bedside light was still switched on. She turned it off, snuggled down beneath the bedclothes and went to sleep.

CHAPTER TWENTY FOUR

Gerald, the man from the commercial department of the estate agents for which Derek worked had telephoned her early the following morning. He sounded excited. When he picked her up in the Mettleham Grand Hotel foyer an hour later he still sounded excited. If he had been a woman he would have been described as `bubbly'. He wore a cheap suit which didn't fit him terribly well but didn't look as bad on him as it might have done because he wore it with an expensive shirt, a silk tie and a pair of what looked like expensive Italian loafers with gold coloured buckles on the sides. He had a chunky, gold coloured bracelet on his right wrist and a chunky gold coloured watch on his left wrist. He smiled a lot and smelt of something unusually delicate which reminded Mrs Caldicot more of a woman's perfume than a man's aftershave. She thought he looked like a cross between a gigolo and a second-hand car salesman, and when he took her arm as they walked out to his car she was conscious of, and secretly rather enjoyed, disapproving looks from a gaggle of matronly and arthritic women who were clambering out of a mini bus.

`I've got just the place for you,' he promised her as he drove furiously through the early morning traffic. He seemed unusually fond of changing gear and kept one hand permanently resting on a shortened gear stick which was topped with a polished walnut sphere. `You'll love it! It only came on the market yesterday afternoon.' His car had a tiny air freshener hanging from the driving mirror and a `No Smoking' notice stuck to the front of the glove compartment. The air freshener reminded her of Mr Caldicot for it, too, made the car smell rather like a public lavatory. The car was spotless inside, without so much as a sweet paper on the floor.

`The important thing is that it must have enough rooms,' said Mrs Caldicot quite firmly.

`Oh, this place has got absolutely oceans of space!' Gerald assured her. He turned and beamed at her and looked back at the road just in time to avoid a head on collision with a double decker bus. `You'll love it!' he promised.

`I'm sure I will!' agreed Mrs Caldicot, digging her fingernails into the car's fake velour upholstery. She closed her eyes as they seemed to head straight for an elderly and innocent pedestrian who had recklessly chosen that moment to attempt a crossing of the road. She wondered why she had felt safe with Jenkins, whose driving could hardly be described as cautious, while she felt distinctly unsafe with Gerald at the wheel.

`Lovely secluded grounds, emergency fire escape and fitted carpets throughout,' said Gerald, as excited as if he himself found these advantages irresistible.

Rather tentatively Mrs Caldicot opened her eyes. There had been no sudden scream and no interruption to their progress but despite the absence of this expected evidence of motorised manslaughter she had still half expected to see the pedestrian draped across the bonnet and the windscreen spattered with blood.   `That's nice,' she said, surprised at how calm her voice sounded.

`Here we are!' said Gerald, a few moments later, driving in through the absurdly gothic iron gates which guarded the driveway up to The Twilight Years Rest Home.

***

Mr Fuller-Hawksmoor, the former proprietor of The Twilight Years Rest Home, and Mrs Caldicot's hapless adversary in the now famous Cabbage War, had suffered a deadly blow when Mrs Caldicot and her followers had walked out.

Without their weekly payments splashing into his bank account he had quite quickly found himself unable to satisfy the bank's insatiable demand for cash. What made things even worse was the fact that after Mrs Caldicot's appearances on television his previously untarnished reputation as a caring individual (untarnished only because no one had cared enough to make the effort to tarnish it) had been besmirched so badly that no other old people had been prepared to enter through the stuccoed portals of The Twilight Years Rest Home. Without in any way meaning to, Mrs Caldicot had succeeded in ruining her former host. The bank, the true owners of The Twilight Years Rest Home, had foreclosed with all the sensitivity and remorse of a boa constrictor swallowing its prey. The few remaining disabled and incontinent residents had moved out and onwards to cleaner sheets elsewhere, and Mr Fuller-Hawksmoor had spent a dull and unproductive morning at the local unemployment exchange struggling quite unsuccessfully to persuade a 16-year-old girl with halitosis of anaesthetic proportions that `Nursing Home Proprietor' was an acceptable and acknowledged occupation.

`How much do you want for it?' asked Mrs Caldicot.

Gerald, standing next to her on the gravel turning circle beneath the front door, tossed the keys to the front door up into the air and almost caught them. `Don't you want to see inside?'

He bent down and picked up the keys. He was not in the slightest bit embarrassed by this example of fate in action.

`It's just what I'm looking for,' said Mrs Caldicot. `How much?'

Gerald went back to his car, brought a briefcase from the back seat, opened it and took out a printed brochure which had a space where there ought to have been a photograph of the home. He put the briefcase down on the ground.

`We haven't got the photos back from the printer yet,' he apologised. He handed the brochure to Mrs Caldicot and pointed to the price.

`How much would the monthly payments be on that?' she asked.

Gerald, bent down, took a calculator out of his briefcase and pressed the keys a few times. Then he held the calculator up so that Mrs Caldicot could see its tiny screen.

Mrs Caldicot did some quick calculations of her own. It was much less than a quarter of what they were paying to stay in the Mettleham Grand Hotel.

`That's far too much,' she said, surprising herself by her shamelessness. She made a counter offer.

`I'll have to get back to you on that,' said Gerald frowning.

`I'd like to see inside now, please,' said Mrs Caldicot.

`Of course!' agreed Gerald, as though as it were the most natural thing in the world for a client to make an offer to buy a property and then to ask to look round it. He picked up his briefcase and took out a mobile phone. `If you don't mind looking around by yourself I could ring the bank and see what they say to your offer...' he suggested, keen to strike while Mrs Caldicot's iron was hot. He opened the front door as he spoke.

`That's a good idea,' said Mrs Caldicot, suddenly overwhelmed by a barrage of memories, most of them unpleasant. She tried to smile at him but no smile would come. She disappeared inside the building, stepping over the inevitable pile of leaflets, free newspapers and unsolicited mail which is tipped through the letterbox of any empty or abandoned building within hours of the previous owner's exit, and wondered how long it would take for the smell of cabbage to disappear. Maybe, she thought, she could festoon the whole building with little disinfectant air fresheners like the one hanging from Gerald's driving mirror.

It seemed strange to be back.

She wandered around and it rather reminded her of the Marie Celeste. The carpets, curtains and furniture were all just as they were when she had left. In the living room there was an open copy of the *Radio Times* lying on the seat of a green, plastic covered easy chair. In the dining room the salt and pepper containers were still standing in the middle of all the tables. A few assorted catering tins and boxes of unwanted food stood on the shelves in the kitchen. A tabloid newspaper, neatly folded, lay on top of the refrigerator. In the bedroom which she had shared with her two friends there was a metal kidney dish on a bedside table and a bottle of pills had been abandoned on the mantelpiece. These small physical memories made it look as though the residents had been spirited away by aliens, leaving everything behind them as it had been.

Mrs Caldicot stood for a moment and then heard a noise from down below.

`Hello! Mrs Caldicot? I've got some good news for you!' she heard Gerald say. Mrs Caldicot walked down the stairs towards him. Still clutching his mobile phone he had stepped into the hallway.

`The bank has accepted your offer,' said Gerald. `I didn't think they would but I put in a good word for you...'

`That's very kind of you,' thought Mrs Caldicot who didn't believe him for an instant. `I don't believe you for an instant!' she said, laughing.

Gerald, who was not in the slightest embarrassed by this, smiled at her.

`Take your time looking round,' he said. `I'll take you back to your hotel when you've finished.'

`That's very kind of you,' smiled Mrs Caldicot, who rather thought she might be pushing her luck to accept another ride in Gerald's disinfected vehicle, `but I'd quite like the walk.'

CHAPTER TWENTY FIVE

It took the estate agents, the banks and the lawyers a week to make all the arrangements so that Mrs Caldicot and her friends could move back into what had, in its previous incarnation, been known as The Twilight Years Rest Home. It took Mrs Caldicot another week to arrange for all the existing furniture in the building to be taken away and sold at auction; for a team of decorators to paint the whole of the inside of the building and for a supply of new furniture to be delivered. While she waited for these improvements to be made Mrs Caldicot traced all the disabled and incontinent former residents of The Twilight Years Rest Home and told them all that they could, if they wanted to, come back to stay with her and the other residents.

The careful, cautious and indomitably pessimistic Derek had insisted that the whole process would inevitably take at least a month to six weeks to complete but Mrs Caldicot had succeeded in speeding things up by the simple expedient of issuing an ultimatum.

`If we aren't moving into the building within two weeks the whole deal is off,' she had told Gerald, and because she had meant it Gerald had believed her. Anxious not to lose his commission Gerald had convinced the solicitors and bankers of Mrs Caldicot's determination. Since they, in their turn, were also keen not to lose their hefty fees, the unnecessary administrative and bureaucratic delays which normally hinder any legal process were suddenly dismissed for what they are (unnecessary administrative and bureaucratic delays) by the only people who have the power to push them aside: the administrators and bureaucrats who had created them in the first place. Mrs Caldicot's appearances on television had given her a strong image which she knew was undeserved, but fortunately this knowledge was not widely shared.

To begin with Miss Nightingale, Mrs Peterborough and the others were more than a touch reluctant to leave the Mettleham Grand Hotel. They had grown to like living there; having become particularly fond of the Sports and Leisure Complex. Mrs Caldicot had, however, managed to overcome their resistance by promising them that they would have their own leisure and fitness centre built onto the side of the building.

'It won't be run like a nursing home,' she told them. 'You'll all be part owners. It'll be a cooperative venture!'

Mrs Caldicot organised interviews for staff and hired a chef, a housekeeper, two waiters and a more than adequate complement of nursing and cleaning staff. She told the housekeeper that she wanted the waiters to wear black suits, white shirts and black ties while the nurses had to wear proper nursing uniforms.

'You don't know what you're taking on!' Derek kept insisting gloomily, but Mrs Caldicot knew exactly what she was taking on and was excited rather than alarmed by it all. She discovered, to her delight, that the money they had been paying as rent to The Twilight Years Rest Home would enable them to live in comparative luxury.

'Will we have a Jack Oozy?' asked Miss Nightingale, who had grown exceedingly partial to a daily bubble bath.

'We certainly will!' Mrs Caldicot assured her.

'And exercise bicycles?'

'Definitely!'

'With bells?'

'Of course!'

'Of course!' said Mrs Peterborough firmly.

The opposition to the move, in truth never anything more than a hint of apprehension, faded quickly into a memory and in due course Mrs Caldicot and her followers moved out of their hotel and back into what was known as The Twilight Years Rest Home.

When their hired coach (Oppenshaw's Char-a-bancs: No Journey Too Short with driver Ted) turned into the drive and passed through the ornate iron gates, the returning residents cheered as they saw the sign which Mrs Caldicot had had specially painted and erected.

'Home Sweet Home' it said in letters two feet high. Underneath, in only slightly smaller letters, were the words 'No Cabbage Allowed'.

It was a victory and a return of which Napoleon himself would have been proud.

The Beginning

You can follow Mrs Caldicot's further adventures in Vernon Coleman's second novel about Mrs Caldicot. The title of the sequel to *Mrs Caldicot's Cabbage War* is *Mrs Caldicot's Knickerbocker Glory*. Other books about Mrs Caldicot include *Mrs Caldicot's Oyster Parade* and *Mrs Caldicot's Turkish Delight*.

Printed in Great Britain
by Amazon

43141939R00087